ITEM 101

BEN SIMON LAZARUS

Item 101

A dystopian social experiment.

Published by Finesse Literary Press:

Finesseliterarypress.com

Written by; Ben Simon Lazarus

Edited by;

Daniel De K.

TABLE OF CONTENTS

CHAPTER 1
CONCEPTUALIZATION

As the day dawned, the critical work was about to start in this mysterious experimental laboratory, located in the heart of Nevada, USA. The mood inside the humid solitary chamber was rather gloomy. The four concrete walls merely represented a physical barrier that separated any individual in this space from the rest of humanity. The daunting aesthetic of the tall wooden doors to the south welcomed one to a new realm of human existence – one of total isolation that led to a fresh sense of normality. Additionally, the sinister darkness in the room reflected the mood it encapsulated – a constant shadow of lifelessness. A single flickering light bulb, hanging from the ceiling fan, provided illumination that would otherwise have come from the only window, a boarded up rectangular pane of dusty and grimy glass in the eastern wall. All in all, this dreary atmosphere defied the perception of pleasure. The only joy in here was in the work that was meticulously carried out from sunrise to sunset each day.

The place hadn't always been a laboratory. In the distant past it used to be an old dilapidated home, restructured for the purpose of conducting tests and experiments.

At exactly 6:15 a.m. an elderly man pushed the creaking doors open with some effort. Ignoring the strong mildew odor, as it was something he'd become accustomed to by now. He straightened his long white robe while looking around, mentally strategizing the start of his day.

After standing like this in the deafening silence for two or three minutes, the man closed the doors and then gradually approached his workstation. Even though he wasn't wearing any shoes, the floorboards still squeaked intensely under his bare feet. Pulling a weary wooden chair out from underneath an equally weary desk, he sat down with a sharp intake of breath.

The man started rocking back and forth on the chair in pulsing motions. He interlocked his fingers and then began to whisper something to himself, almost humming the sounds. If anyone was listening they would have sensed a certain kind of rhythmic sequence in his voice. It sounded like a series of random numbers and letters, but if there had been any bystanders in the laboratory they wouldn't have been able to properly distinguish the pattern that was hidden inside the man's brilliant mind.

Then, all of a sudden, just as he seemed to evolve into a flowing scientific tango of some sorts, his breathing pattern drastically changed as his heartbeat rapidly increased to an unusually fast rate. His eyes opened wide and he raised a bushy white eyebrow before abruptly ceasing his rocking motions.

Burying his head in the palms of his hands, the man began to chuckle, now sounding like a much younger version of himself. Then he swiftly rose to his feet and enthusiastically shouted, 'It can't be!'

He hurried across the room to an enormous chalkboard filled with mathematical equations, reminiscent of an unknown dialect. Following only a slight hesitation, the man flipped the chalkboard over to uncover the blank side. There was another brief pause while he attempted to gather his compartmentalized thoughts into a single logical scientific scheme. Then, as fast as he could, he scribbled down what appeared to be a random combination of characters, all while speaking them out loud. In an attempt to articulate his fragmented thoughts, he now also picked up the eraser in his other hand, rubbing out some numbers and replacing them with others as he went along.

The scribbling became increasingly intensified. Whilst continuing to write, he began to sweat profusely and started stuttering nervously. At some point during this frantic exercise he put down the eraser and used the back of his hand to wipe his forehead, where drops of perspiration were trickling down onto the protective goggles covering his eyes. After running his moist hand through his wavy white hair, he took off his thick white robe and then sucked in a deep breath of air to calm himself down.

Finally, he removed his goggles and shrieked, 'Could it be?'

Out of the blue, the professor suddenly heard a noise coming from the direction of the laboratory's doors. Startled, he hopped involuntarily, then threw the chalk and the goggles in the air and belted out something that sounded like a mix between a growl and a yelp.

'Good evening, Professor Alberstein,' said a cheerful female voice while whistling leisurely.

'Oh, it's just you, Carla,' the professor replied, turning on his heels to face her.

Dr Carla Williams was well groomed and presented herself beautifully. Her mere presence and the aura she radiated made her stick out like a sore thumb in this dull environment.

'Please don't distract me right now,' the professor urged. 'I'm in the middle of doing something incredibly important.' He pointed to the corner of the room and added in a demanding tone, 'Stand there for a moment and don't speak. I've got a brainwave going and I don't want to lose my train of thoughts.'

Carla's facial expression made a hundred-and-eighty degree turn. Her bright smile quickly changed into a confused smirk as she gazed intensely at the professor. He didn't look back at her; he was too busy trying to maintain his state of deep contemplation.

With reluctance, Carla walked towards the corner he had indicated. She came to a halt next to the specialist equipment or, more specifically, the area where the spectrophotometers, calorimeters and conditioning chambers were kept. She tried her utmost best not to touch anything or bump against any piece of apparatus. The last thing she wanted to do now was to make a noise to distract the professor from his work. Carla knew she'd have to deal with his wrath, she had seen him in this state before. Therefore, she just stood still and waited as patiently as she could for clarification regarding the hieroglyphs on the chalkboard. Whilst doing so her mind was racing, attempting to figure out what on earth the professor was doing.

A few anxiety-ridden minutes went by and then Carla felt that it was the right time to try and break the silence. 'Professor,' she said hesitantly, 'anything I can help you out with?'

'Quiet!' the professor barked in a resentful voice.

Her face turned bright red with embarrassment, indicating a realisation of the superiority complex in the laboratory. She stood awkwardly, with her narrow shoulders drooping and her slender arms folded across her chest, still watching the professor expectantly.

The professor rolled the piece of chalk between his fingers and then carefully placed it on the board's stand. Taking two long steps back, he exhaled noisily and then stared in Carla's direction while pointing his index finger towards his work board. Carla gave him a look of utter confusion as she gazed at the nonsensical algorithm that she recognised as nothing more than squiggles on a chalkboard.

'Carla, don't you see?' he asked her with genuine elation written across his face.

Carla looked at the professor intently and he quickly met her gaze. Noticing the solemnity in his eyes and realising the uncharacteristic nature of his actions, she asked, 'Is there something wrong, Professor? You've seemed a little off from the moment I walked through the door.'

'Wrong?' he answered, frowning. Then he started laughing uncontrollably while Carla was looking on, perplexed. When Professor Alberstein finally managed to compose himself, he said while grinning from ear to ear. 'As a matter of fact, my dear Carla, things have never been this right in my entire life!'

She dropped her chin to her chest, trying to process everything she had just seen and heard. It didn't seem like she shared the professor's excitement, purely because she had no clue what he was going on about. In fact, Carla Williams was left with a somewhat depressed look, as the professor's strange behavior was bothering her a great deal.

'Look at me, Carla,' the professor now instructed. 'I'll explain in simplistic terms, so even you can understand.' He paused to clear his throat and then said, 'So, I've just run through the figures for the millionth time, and they finally added up.'

'What do you mean?' she responded, raising her plucked eyebrows.

'I've determined that *it's* practically viable,' the professor whispered dramatically.

Carla looked up in astonishment. She opened her mouth to speak, but her vocal chords momentarily refused to produce the words. She licked her dry lips and finally responded with, 'Wait, you don't mean?'

The professor nodded.

'I-I-I-Item 101?' she stammered. 'But, I, I just don't understand. How is that possible, Professor?'

'I've projected that by strictly following my mathematical formula, with applied physics, and the right mechanical craftsmanship, Item 101 can be engineered to carry out its functions proficiently,' the professor said confidently.

Carla stood there, stunned. She was left absolutely speechless, having no idea of what to say in response to the professor's remarkable discovery.

CHAPTER 2
POWERSOURCE

It was a lovely room, simplistic yet quite elegant. Inspired by the Victorian London era, the marble-like white bricks in the high walls gave the interior a feeling of utter cleanliness. The tapestry on the floor was sleek and indicated the jouissance of the owners. A few old pieces of neatly arranged furniture were worn but aesthetically gorgeous due to their classy antique look. Cream-coloured curtains - embroidered with luxurious linen - covered two large bay windows and a stone fireplace in the corner gave the place a warm, homely feel on this bright and crisp winter morning. A stylish granite mantlepiece atop the fireplace displayed framed black-and-white family photographs; the faces an ubiquitous statement of joyousness.

A day had passed since Professor Alberstein's major breakthrough and Carla Williams was sitting in her favourite armchair, gazing at the flickering flames. As she was about to take the first sip of her morning coffee she heard the faint footsteps of her husband coming down the stairs. Shifting her gaze from the fireplace to the door she called, 'Jared, darling, would you like a coffee?'

'Yes please, honey,' he responded as he entered the living room.

Carla leaned over to place her mug on the coffee table, with all intentions to make her way to the kitchen to put the kettle on. Whilst doing so, she unexpectedly heard a loud and aggressive banging on the front door. She jumped up in surprise and lost her grip on the coffee mug's handle. The mug, filled to the brim with strong coffee, fell to the floor and Carla shrieked loudly as the steaming hot liquid splashed over her feet. Looking down, she noticed that her usually spotless white carpet was now stained with a dark brown tint. She was instantly annoyed. It really didn't match the rest of her living room's pristine decorations.

Meanwhile, Jared had hurried to the front door but still seemed hesitant to answer the call.

'Open up immediately!' a man shouted, whilst continuing to smash his fists on the outside surface of the door.

'All right, calm down,' Jared Williams replied as he tentatively opened the door to a slight crack.

Peeking his head through the gap, he saw Professor Alberstein on their doorstep. The bewildered old man was wearing only his signature white robe, nothing else, not even shoes. But, then again, the professor *never* wore shoes. It wasn't raining but his face was dripping wet. He also had dark circles under his eyes, Jared noticed, and his breath was racing. His foul body odour reeked to high heavens.

Without warning, the professor pushed the door open and stormed inside. The force knocked poor Jared off his feet and he fell to the ground like a sack of potatoes. He looked up and saw the shadow of the almost scary professor's figure above him. 'Don't hurt me,' he pleaded in a desperate cry.

'Oh, please,' said the professor, chuckling wittingly. 'You're not worth hurting.'

'How extremely inappropriate, Professor!' This coming from Carla, who was still standing on the stained carpet in the living room. She threw her arms in the air while looking down at the spilt coffee. 'Look at what you've done here,' she said, then turned her attention back to the old man in the doorway. 'And what are you doing at my house on a Sunday morning?' she asked with a puzzled expression on her pale face.

'Just be quiet and hear me out,' replied the professor, walking into the living room in determined strides.

Jared tried to interrupt but before he could do so the professor pointed a bony finger at him and said, 'That goes for you too, Mr Williams.'

The owners of the house only now observed that Professor Alberstein was cradling a large bump, giving the impression that he was hiding something beneath his robe.

As if reading their minds, the professor undid his robe's knot and produced a strange contraption which he put down on the coffee table. Jared and Carla were taken back. Neither of them had seen anything like this before.

The device was in the shape of a capsule and portrayed the direct point at which modern 1980s technology and human innovation met. It had an unsettling soft-touch look; a kind of mucilaginous consistency. The capsule was predominantly green in colour, with an odd turquoise undertone. On top it was fitted with a type of metal satellite dish, slowly revolving in a continuous clockwise direction. The device also contained several multi-coloured lights on the side, flashing on and off in inconsistent strobes. Jared and Carla could hear that it emitted peculiar sounds, beeping and whirring in an otherworldly way. But what was perhaps most striking was the orifice at the bottom, dense with an array of wires, comparable to roots.

'I want to give you a demonstration,' the professor now said. 'Watch closely.'

He started by transferring a pipette of thick fluid from one large tube into an opening at the top of the device. He ensued purposeful chemical decontamination as the potion hissed and bubbled. A plasma light then began to gleam in the centre, underneath the metallic layer covering it. The machinery ticked and clanked noisily while the wires at the bottom of the capsule sparked and buzzed with energy.

Absolutely gobsmacked, the married couple stepped back, their eyes lighting up with curiosity and their jaws dropping in astonishment.

'Carla, I think you'll want to be seated for what I'm about to tell you,' said the professor, clasping his hands together. 'Here, as you can probably derive, we have a prototype for the nucleus of Item 101.' He paused to allow the ground-breaking information to sink in before continuing in a confident tone. 'It's the brain of the device, if you will, and here we have it. Please admire it in all its glory.'

A tear trickled down Carla's cheek. 'It's beautiful,' she admitted in a trembling voice. At the same time, Jared cringed at the device, giving it a sinister glare of disapproval.

'However,' Professor Alberstein resumed, 'we need to link this up to a mainframe for it to function to our scientific requirements.'

'Okay, that makes sense,' Carla responded, nodding her head in comprehension. Then her face turned quizzical. 'So, have you built this mainframe yet, Professor?'

'Yes, I've completed it,' the professor assured her. 'It's in the laboratory, I couldn't bring it here because it's a rather large device and portability isn't viable at this time.'

'Oh, right, I understand,' Carla said, once again nodding. 'So, why don't we head down there right now and test it out?' she asked excitedly.

'Impossible!' he replied in a loud grunt.

Jared and Cara looked at each other in confusion.

The professor then laughed at Carla's question, a question that he appeared to be finding somewhat irrelevant. 'The energy the nucleus generates isn't enough to power the mainframe,' he stated matter-of-factly. 'We need to use this in combination with an alternative, more powerful energy source.'

'You mean?' Carla said, furrowing her brow.

'Plutonium,' they both murmured at the same time.

'Exactly!' Professor Alberstein confirmed. 'And as my assistant, you're going to help me get it.'

Carla rolled her eyes and sighed intently.

CHAPTER 3
DIVORCE BELLS RINGING

The sun set over a perplexing day and the twilight of dusk gradually gave way to the striking assembly of stars in the vast expanse of the night sky. Carla Williams was quite exhausted after a stressful weekend filled with surprises. It was now time to embrace the tranquility of the night, so she just stood out on the front porch and gazed at the starry atmosphere, deep in her own thoughts.

Even though she had seen the beauty of nightfall from her home so many times before, it still amazed her how stunning the milky way and the bright illumination of a full moon could be. After a while of pondering like this Carla started feeling weary-eyed and decided it was time to resign to bed. With one last momentary peek at her favourite star sign she quietly made her way inside and locked the front door.

Minutes later she entered her cosy bedroom upstairs. Like her, Jared was already in his pyjamas, propped up in bed with his bedside lamp on. He was balancing a cup of tea in one hand while holding the paperback book he was reading in the other.

Carla looked at her husband without saying anything. She didn't want to disturb him. Jared had a concerned look upon his face and – as he peered over his book to stare at her – his eyes spelled judgement and disapproval. Both of them refused to break the silence.

Carla plunged onto the mattress and then got into a comfortable position by turning on her side, with her back facing Jared. She started rummaging through her bedside drawer and retrieved a roll of white dressing and a tube of burn care cream. She applied the cream and cautiously wrapped the covering around her foot, then returned the two items to the drawer and climbed in under the fluffy duvet.

She was about to shut her eyes when Jared said, 'Okay, 'I'm just going to come out and say it'.

'Go on then,' Carla told him, sounding cold and distant.

'You're not actually crazy enough to go through with this, are you?' Jared asked.

Carla turned around to face him. 'With what?' she said with a frown, acting as if she didn't have the slightest idea what he was talking about.

'Don't play dumb with me,' Jared said bluntly. 'You know, the professor's *mission* to find plutonium.'

'How can you judge someone you don't even know?' Carla asked. She sat up in the bed and continued to speak with animated hands. 'Look, I'm not even sure what the plan is yet. But the way I know professor Alberstein he would never put me in any danger.'

'Wouldn't put you in any danger?' Jared said incredulously. 'Are you even listening to yourself, Carla? I tell you what: I don't trust this so-called *professor* as far as I could throw him. '

She heaved an exhausted sigh. 'You just don't get it, do you, Jared? The only reason why you're upset is that you don't understand the professor.'

'What's there to understand about him? He's a nut!' Jared shouted, raising his voice to emphasise his point.

'Everything he does is extremely calculated,' Carla responded in a calm voice. 'He thinks like a physicist and he is always planning everything on a mathematical level. You simply don't see him for the genius he is.' When Jared didn't have any comeback to this statement she sneeringly added, 'But someone like you wouldn't understand something like that, would you?'

'Oh,' Jared said, lacing his reply with a sarcastic chuckle. 'So the way you're speaking to me right now… I suppose that's the way the professor speaks to you as well.' He made a snorting sound before resuming. 'Look at what you've become, Carla. You're basically turning into him.'

Carla folded her arms across her chest in sheer frustration. 'How dare you say that to me?' she demanded with a serious look in her emerald green eyes.

'Oh, so now I'm not smart enough to understand, huh?' Jared countered. 'And, yet, I'm the only person who sees through his charade? You realise he's doing all of this only for himself, right?'

'He's doing it for humanity!' Carla cried out, expressing her annoyance.

Jared shook his head in disagreement. 'You're blind you know, Carla,' he said loudly. 'You're nothing but a fool. You've complained to me about the professor countless times before. You always talk about how he patronises you and degrades you at the workplace. He speaks to you like you're not the clever, beautiful doctor I know you are. He doesn't respect you at all.' Jared's face was growing red and he inhaled deeply to catch his breath.

'I see what you're doing,' Carla replied in a firm voice. 'I know you too well. I see right through you, Jared.

You're trying to manipulate me. And this time, I'm not falling for it.'

Jared, who was by now rather fed up with the conversation, cleared his throat and then said, 'Okay, so let me tell you how it's going to work then, loud and clear. I won't sugar coat it for you any longer, so listen to me and listen good, Carla, dear. From now on you are not going to have any association with this man anymore. He is crazy and dangerous! I forbid you from ever seeing him again. I'll get you a job at my dad's real-estate firm and we can live happily ever after, do you understand?'

Carla couldn't believe her ears. How could he say that to her? She glared at Jared in visible disgust. After taking a minute to decide on how to respond, she unwillingly broke down in tears. Holding her head in her hands, she started sobbing relentlessly.

While Jared did nothing to comfort her, Carla slowly regained her composure to a point where she could actually get a few words out. She locked eyes with her husband and said, 'Oh, you forbid me, do you? You think you can tell me what to do? It's my life, not yours, Jared. The invention of Item 101 will change everything forever. I have dedicated my entire career for this breakthrough. And you're telling me to just give up now?' Carla was close to shouting and her mind was in a total frenzy. 'You know what, Jared?' she continued.

'If you want to control me, you're not someone I want to spend the rest of my life with anymore. This has all been a big mistake. I'm moving in with my parents, I never want to speak to you again.'

She jumped out of bed and ripped open her wardrobe's doors.

After pulling two luggage cases from underneath the bed, she stuffed all her clothing into them (without neatly folding anything like she always did) and then proceeded to add her other possessions from the nightstand and the en-suite bathroom into the suitcases: jewellery, make-up, toiletries, hairbrushes, basically everything that didn't belong to Jared. During all of this neither of them said a single word.

No more than fifteen minutes later, Carla stormed down the stairs and out the front door in a tantrum.

Moments after she had slammed the door shut behind her, Jared fetched his passport from his dressing table's drawer and hurried downstairs where the only telephone in the house was located. He opened the phonebook on the kitchen counter and looked up the airport's number for bookings and reservations.

When the operator answered, he said, 'Good evening, ma'am, this is Jared Williams speaking. I need to make a booking on the next flight from Nevada to Washington D.C.'

'Yes, Mr Williams,' she replied in a squeaky voice. 'No problem at all, sir. The next flight out leaves in a matter of hours. We have a number of seats available, the manifest isn't even half full.'

'Perfect,' he said, 'I'll book a taxi to the airport right away.' Once he had thanked the operator for her assistance, he hung up the phone and called for a cab.

CHAPTER 4
LIKE STEALING CANDY
FROM A BABY

It was the evening of Jared and Carla's separation and it was a crisp night in a deserted land.

The harsh sunlight of daytime had subsided and the darkness was now expanding upon the undulating desert for miles on end. The burning sensation of the torrid heat earlier gradually turned into a slight breeze caressing the night air. Here, the cosmic surface of the barren land stretched as far as the imagination could wonder. Predominantly white sand and black skies defined the elementary scenery of this expanse at night time. Total serenity and calmness radiated from a truly unexploited region of nature, spanning across an area as far as the human eye could see. Had there been someone around, each of their steps would sink their feet into the powdery sand, however, there was no form of life in sight, not even a lone cactus plant. These treacherous desert conditions simply made the space uninhabitable and the whole zone seemed completely untouched by humanity; desolate and lonesome.

Situated somewhere in the middle of this desert, a bright red light on a tall metal pole suddenly started blinking rapidly. The light was located near a mysterious road and its beaming flickers were now also illuminating an entire courtyard below. Whilst flashing cherry-red beams, the light revealed that the mysterious road didn't wind or bend at all. It was long and straight and stretched across a vast area of sand, miles into the distance. It was like the road never ended and had no start or finish points. There were large sign boards reading *Classified Vehicles Only* at regular intervals, clearly forbidding any commercial cars to travel around on this section of tarmac.

A relentless siren then went off. It was a loud, looping noise with the ability to almost pierce an eardrum with its seriously high-pitched tone. The siren was accompanied by a voice-over announcement, sending out a repeated message that there was now an emergency situation underway. 'Intruder alert! Intruder alert!' the voice-over kept on blaring. Ground soldiers on foot were triggered into action and ran into the courtyard, searching for a perpetrator of some kind. They were carrying various electronic devices and weaponry, pointing in every direction of the perimeter surrounding the premises. These men were professionals; every corner was covered. The combination of their shining flashlights, along with the red light, uncovered another sign near the courtyard entrance. This sign read *AREA 51, Classified Personnel Only.*

Sergeant Major General Fisher was accompanied by his colleague and deputy, Command Sergeant Major Earl, in the courtyard compound. They were sitting together in a luxurious office, smoking fat Cuban cigars. They looked at each other in confusion as they heard the siren go off.

Earl quickly spoke into his two-way radio and then turned to face Fisher. 'Major General,' he said nervously. 'We have a report that someone has triggered an alarm in sector 58.'

'Sector 58?' Fisher replied, frowning. 'How is that possible? I was under the impression that these entry alarm codes could not be cracked. It would take someone with superhuman abilities, a super genius if you will, to figure out how to breach our system and gain entry.'

'Yes, I know, sir,' Earl responded, extinguishing his cigar in a ceramic ashtray on the table. 'And what is even more concerning is that the report also stated the plutonium in the secure store has gone missing.'

'Lock down the premises immediately!' Fisher ordered, rising to his feet in a panic.

Command Sergeant Major Earl leaned over to the control panel beside his chair and pressed a sizable red button that initiated an electronic quarantine in the courtyard. All points of entry and exit were instantly locked.

There were two guards standing outside the perimeter of the establishment. 'What is that noise, Private?' one of them asked the other, looking in the direction where a low, droning sound was coming from.

Professor Alberstein was running towards a bulky pickup truck on a nearby road in the desert. 'GO! GO! GO!' he shouted as he finally reached the back of the truck and hurled himself over the tailgate and onto the floor panel. He was panting quite heavily and rolled onto his back while the truck gained speed, nearly slipping off the road and onto the sand.

'I don't know,' the other guard responded. 'It sounds like an engine of some sorts.' He stared into the dark distance and then said, 'Wait, is it just me or are there faint lights over there by the road?'

The other military guard squinted his eyes and looked in the direction the other guard was facing. 'I think you're right!' he said loudly. They both aimed their rifles at the dim lights and one of them shouted, 'Fire!' thereafter they started shooting.

The glass pane in the truck's back window was smashed in with the first bullet. A woman in the front screamed loudly and then shouted, 'What was that?'

'Someone is shooting at us!' the professor shouted back.

'Aim at the tires,' one of the uniformed guards instructed as they continued shooting. The thick smell of gunpowder hung in the air and a cloud of blue smoke had now formed around them.

The driver in the truck's cabin said, 'I think I have an idea, hold on.'

'This is no time for one of your flawed ideas!' Professor Alberstein replied in a strained voice.

The driver promptly switched off the truck's headlights and then the professor yelled, 'What are you doing, are you crazy? You won't be able to see anything!'

Ignoring the professor's comments, the driver gripped the steering wheel tight and kept the vehicle in a straight line as they edged further away from the danger.

Then the bullets stopped flying. 'We lost them, Private,' one of the guards said in frustration.

'Damn it!' the other replied. They both dropped their guns to the ground, shuddering. They knew that Sergeant Major General Fisher was going to have their heads on plate for this mishap.

'Pretty smart, Carla,' the professor said once they were out of harm's way. Carla had a smile on her face (actually it was more like a cocky smirk) as she switched the lights back on and kept driving as fast as she could down the desert road, back to civilization. On their route back home, she briefly considered telling Professor Alberstein about the incident that had occurred between herself and her husband, but in the end decided against it. The professor had enough other worries in his head, she figured.

Back at the military compound Fisher and Earl were studying recorded CCTV footage of the white-haired man running from the storage buildings. Fisher banged his balled fists on the table and looked at Earl. 'Who on earth is this guy?' he asked angrily. 'And who is he working with? Call the FBI and put him on the most wanted list! Inform the president! I want you to find him, dead or alive. Make it happen now, Earl!'

By the time the professor and Carla had completed their long and treacherous drive back from Area 51, it was already well into the early hours of the morning. Before they parted ways to finally get a wink of sleep, the professor reiterated that 'time was of the essence'. He then looked at her with a stern expression on his face when he added, 'Our work must commence not long after sunrise, Carla. I will meet you at the laboratory at 8:30 a.m. sharp, all right?'

'Got it, Professor Alberstein,' she replied, yawning behind her hand.

The professor and Carla went back to their respective homes on the outskirts of Nevada and both fell asleep as soon as their heads hit the pillows. It was already 3:30 a.m. so they weren't in for much rest.

CHAPTER 5
JARED'S JOURNEY

Jared was awoken by a slight thud when the passenger plane touched down on the tarmac runway in Washington D.C. He rubbed his eyes with his fists and then looked out the tiny window. The blue skies bequeathed anew, though dotted with puffy clouds as the nascent sun rose shortly after 6:30 a.m.

Snapping out of his disoriented and hazy state, Jared now had an element of seriousness and focus on his face. His eyes felt weary and he was showing faint signs of physical and mental exhaustion but he remained quiet and subdued, conveniently ignoring the other passengers.

After disembarking and passing through the security checkpoint, Jared walked out of the terminal building just as it began to rain. While covering his head with his briefcase he hurried along the wet sidewalk, flagging down a taxi. He was successful within seconds.

'White House,' he instructed as he climbed in, 'and you'd better step on it!'

The taxi driver sensed Jared's urgency and sped off with the wipers turned to the fastest setting; there was now a steady patter of raindrops hitting the windshield.

When they arrived at their destination at exactly 9:09 a.m. the rain had stopped. Jared got out of the taxi and beheld the residence and workplace of the most powerful man on the planet. Here, the ominous-looking black gates surrounding the premises separated members of the public from the secrets inside the white walls and tall pillars. The people flocking outside the gates of the White House were mostly tourists taking pictures, but there were also a number of protestors, all shouting and desperately trying to drown out the sounds of those around them.

Now there was one man shouting even louder than everybody else – Jared Williams.

He was using his hands as a makeshift megaphone, cupping them around his mouth to get his message across to the government. He kept on repeating the same words over and over again: 'They're hiding it from you.' 'They've stolen your plutonium.' 'Item 101 is real!'

For the most part Jared was ignored. People tended to simply walk past him like he was another nutcase with some governmental conspiracy theory to throw out there. That was, however, until he caught the eye of one particular individual. This was a bulky male security guard wearing a black suit and dark sunglasses.

At first the guard was only staring from a distance but when he approached Jared and realised what he was saying, he began to panic. Drops of perspiration quickly formed on his forehead and his breath started racing. Lifting his left arm, he spoke into the miniscule microphone in his shirt's cuff in a hoarse whisper. 'I've got an emergency situation here,' he informed the control room.

'What is it, Agent Johnson?' came the high-pitched yet serious voice of a female operator, the sound crackling in his state-of-the-art earpiece.

'I have a middle aged gentleman here who's referencing the Area 51 security breach.'

'How can that be?' the operator responded. Then it sounded like she was speaking to someone else in the control room. Upon returning her attention to the security guard, her voice was even more pressing. 'Agent Johnson,' she said. 'You must detain him immediately. We need to find out everything he knows.'

Agent Johnson walked over to Jared and took him by his elbow. 'Sir, I'm with the FBI,' he said, flashing his identity card in front of Jared's nose. 'I'm going to need you to come with me. Don't make this difficult. If you go against me, I will have to call for backup.'

'No backup needed!' Jared replied cheerfully. 'I'll happily come with you.' This was exactly what he'd hoped would happen. Now he would be able to tell his story to the authorities without having to shout like all these other stupid protestors.

Glaring at Jared in confusion, Agent Johnson proceeded to grip his arm tightly and then steadily guided him through the main gate and into the oval office as more guards followed suit.

The president's personal assistant, Valery Watson, knocked on his door not long after that.

'Come in', he called out.

'Mr President, sir, we've detained a Mr *Jared Williams.* He's here to talk with you.'

'Who on earth is that?' the president said loudly. 'My time is very valuable, don't waste it. Get out of my office, Valery.'

'Mr President, you don't understand!' she bit back firmly. 'This man claims he has information regarding the Area 51 security breach.'

'You can't be serious!' he growled with shock written all across his face. He smacked the surface of his desk with the palm of his hand and then said, 'I'm sorry, Valery. Please send him in immediately.'

CHAPTER 6
WE INTERRUPT THIS PROGRAMME TO BRING YOU AN IMPORTANT MESSAGE FROM…

Back in Nevada, Professor Alberstein and Carla strolled into the laboratory shortly before 8:30 a.m. that morning. With the time difference, this was only a matter of hours after Jared's meeting with the president. Outside, a fresh breeze was blowing and the sky was filled with radiant sun rays, bathing the laboratory in a warm orange-yellow glow. The lack of sleep didn't impact the mood of the two scientists; they were now operating on pure adrenaline and vibrant expectation. For the first time ever it felt as if the perfect weather conditions reflected the mood in the laboratory in a positive way, almost like a deep sweetness resonating from the air and blowing essence into their minds and bodies.

As Carla eased the laboratory doors shut behind her, she was instantly taken aback when her eyes fell upon the outlines of an extremely large object, hidden underneath a canvas sheet in the centre of the room. It was not only the sheer size of it that had drawn her attention, the unknown object was also emitting a loud yet strange monotonous ticking sound.

She looked at the professor with a sly smirk, but before she could even open her mouth to speak, the professor grinned while saying, 'You'll find out in due time, Carla, dear.'

He pulled on a pair of rubber gloves and then approached the nucleus capsule where it was standing beside his workstation's desk. After he'd cautiously picked it up with outstretched arms, the professor placed the capsule on a flattish metal trolley and wheeled it all the way to the covered object in the centre of the floor. Carla stood aside, suddenly understanding the delicacy of the task at hand. She didn't have that same awkward and embarrassed feeling she'd had the last time she was with the professor here in the laboratory. On this occasion she trusted that he knew what was the best course of action to complete their imminent scientific breakthrough.

Professor Alberstein took a deep breath and then pulled the canvas off the object in one swift motion, revealing a steel framed contraption of some sorts. 'Here we have it!' he boasted. 'This is the mainframe. Isn't she magnificent?'

Gazing at the contraption in awe and wonder, Carla gasped. Never before in her life had she seen something so technologically advanced. The exterior frame of the box-shaped mainframe was made of stainless steel and she could see several buttons, knobs and LED lights. The mechanical ticking sound was coming from a cover that was flapping up and down. Through the mysterious transparent panels in the frame Carla could make out a nest of tangled copper wires, transmitting a frictional electrical current that made the machine buzz. The sound reminded her of the electricity pylons running along the field behind her house. The wires inside the mainframe were joined together by small, complicated silver cogs and beyond all of this was a big empty space, the perfect size for the nucleus capsule.

'Pass me the tweezers and the magnifying glass, will you?' Professor Alberstein requested, interrupting Carla's thoughts. She raced over to the work bench and fetched the tools, eager to be of assistance. Once she'd handed them to him, the professor placed the nucleus inside the mainframe and used the tweezers to connect two thick wires together, a red one from the nucleus' orifice and a black one from the mainframe.

'You may want to put on your protective gear now, Carla,' he recommended.

Before she could act, however, there was a bright white spark, so vivid that it resembled a beaming glimmer of light coming from the nucleus. Now that the nucleus was being powered by the mainframe, the professor looked thrilled and muttered something inaudible as he proudly stared at his handiwork with folded arms. The ticking became louder and the cogs began to turn, making a whirring mechanical sound. 'Now for our secret ingredient,' Alberstein said, adding plutonium to the nucleus before shutting the mainframe's flap. The light started growing even brighter and the sparkles it emitted more prominent.

'What on earth is happening here?' Carla asked, her senses intensifying.

Professor Alberstein giggled and she gave a nervous cry as they could see clouds of hazy fog rise from the mainframe and the nucleus. Then, all of a sudden, they were both blown back as a gust came from the complex machinery.

'The energy being emitted!' the professor shouted. 'It's frightening.'

The machine's blast was forceful enough to leave both of them on the floor on their backsides. 'Ouch!' Carla yelled, grasping the elbow she had landed on.

The professor briefly blacked out from the impact before swiftly returning to consciousness. Attempting to regain his composure, he shook his head wildly and then stood up too quickly. After stumbling around in a circle he regained his balance as the smoke cleared away. In his bewilderment, Professor Alberstein was now looking at the contraption in pure amazement. 'My baby!' he cried out, advancing towards the contraption, from then on to be known as Item 101.

Before he or Carla could utter another word, there was an eruption of noise outside the doors.

'It's the Federal Government, open up!' Fisher shouted, leading the charge alongside his colleague, Earl.

The professor ran to the door in a feeble effort to buy a few seconds of time. 'Carla, watch over Item 101!' he said sternly. Still holding her bruised elbow, she did as she was told.

Just like Professor Alberstein had anticipated, it didn't take long for them to smash the doors in. 'Quickly, Carla, disarm the device!' he shouted as soldiers began to spill into the laboratory.

She hastily put on a pair of gloves, then opened the mainframe's flap and grabbed the piece of plutonium from the centre of the nucleus, trying to yank it out with the arm that wasn't in pain. Her grip wasn't strong enough since the plutonium was wedged in, so she proceeded to pull with both her arms. 'Aahh!' she yelled out as the agony intensified in her bruised elbow.

The team of soldiers rapidly rushed into the lab and Fisher, the first one in, jumped onto Carla's back. Carla kept her grip on the stick of plutonium. With the weight of both of their bodies the plutonium finally came loose and the device shut down with a low hum.

'Detain them!' Earl ordered, pointing an angry finger.

'Damn it!' Fisher shouted, smacking the wall with his open hands in pure frustration.

CHAPTER 7
AREA 51

Jared Williams - together with the president and his trusty assistant Valery - were flown from Washington D.C. to Nevada on one of the government's private jets. They were also accompanied by several illustrious White House officials and their personal bodyguards. Everybody on the flight was dressed in formal-wear; the men in suits and shaded glasses, the women in formal blouses and navy trousers.

Dozens of uniformed soldiers and administrative military personnel looked on in astonishment as the jet landed on a special runway next to the main courtyard at Area 51. They all gathered behind the wire fence separating the courtyard from the runway, watching the president as he walked down the airplane's stairs.

'Everyone disperse!' a security guard instructed. When there was now reaction, he blew on a whistle around his neck and then raised his voice to a booming thunder. 'Evacuate the compound right now!'

They all reluctantly flocked towards a row of dome-shaped bunkers, situated in the dry desert on the other side of the courtyard, most of them disappointed not to have the opportunity of meeting the country's highly respected commander-in-chief.

Sergeant Major General Fisher and Command Sergeant Major Earl emerged from the control room building and marched through the runway gate, approaching the jet airliner with stern expressions on their faces. They both shook hands with the president and Fisher said, 'It's good to see you again, Mr President.'

'Good afternoon, gents,' the president greeted. 'Please take me to the location of this Item 101.'

'Certainly, sir,' Earl responded, giving a sharp salute.

The two majors led the way as the president followed, with Valery and Jared and the rest of the entourage shadowing them in the bright sunlight. After walking for about three hundred yards, Earl and Fisher came to a halt on a concrete platform in the middle of the court-yard. Nearly a third of this platform was occupied by Alberstein's strange mainframe/nucleus contraption.

'So this is it?' the president asked, gazing at the gleaming machinery with a finger on his chin. Once he had briefly studied Item 101 from various angles he added, 'Well done for securing this equipment, gentlemen.'

'You're welcome, Mr President,' Fisher replied with a sheepish look on his face.

'Would you like to see a demonstration, sir?' Earl asked.

'Go ahead, please,' said the president.

Sergeant Major General Fisher turned to his left and shouted, 'Bring him in!'

Two broad-shouldered security guards came out of an outbuilding, carrying Professor Alberstein, with his legs dangling across the ground. He was squirming around to free himself but he was unsuccessful – the guards were simply too strong. Their hands were clasped so tightly around his upper arms, it felt as if he was being held in place by two iron vice grips.

'Our top federal scientists couldn't figure out how this machine works,' Earl explained, 'so we've detained the inventor himself.'

'Let me go!' the professor demanded.

Jared stepped out from behind the president and said, 'Well, well, look who it is…' Before Alberstein could respond, he sarcastically added, 'It's nice to see you again, Professor. Lets see if your brains will be able to help you out of this conundrum, shall we?'

'I should have known you were going to be here,' the professor replied in a cynical voice.

Then, as if on cue, two more security guards came through a different door, holding Carla by her shoulders.

'Carla!' Jared exclaimed, his eyes widening in shock. He spun around to face the president and said, 'I told you to only arrest the professor. Release her!'

Carla sneered at her husband while saying, 'I'll never forgive you for this Ja…' Before she could finish her sentence, the guards swiftly taped her mouth shut.

'Professor, talk to us,' said the president. 'What is this machine for and how does it work?'

The professor shook his head violently. 'I'm not giving you any information,' he said through gritted teeth. 'I'd rather die than let you exploit the use of Item 101.'

'We would never exploit its use,' the president assured him.

'I refuse to work with you fools,' the professor stated. There was a bitterness in his tone.

'Let's start with the girl', Command Sergeant Major Earl suggested. His proposal was greeted with a nod of approval from Sergeant Major General Fisher as well as the president. One of the security guards holding Carla pulled his pistol from its holster and pressed the barrel against her right temple. Professor Alberstein and Jared Williams both gulped.

'How about now?' the president asked the professor.

'Do it, you ignorant scientist!' Jared shouted. 'Show us how this thing works.'

'Here's the deal,' Sergeant Major General Fisher said. 'We will use it together, Professor. You win your freedom and no lives are lost. Just give us a short demonstration, okay?'

Command Sergeant Major Earl clenched his jaw. 'That is the best deal you are going to get, Professor Alberstein. I suggest you take it.'

The professor now had a rather disappointed look on his face. The look of a man who had been defeated. He glanced at poor Carla and noticed the absolute fright in her watery eyes. He was genuinely sorry for dragging her into all of this. 'All right, all right, I'll do it,' he eventually said with a loud sigh.

Dropping the professor to the ground, the two guards stepped aside. Alberstein slowly pushed himself to his feet, then dusted off his robe and walked over to the device, acutely aware of the guns pointed at him. He knew they were watching his every move and that any misstep could bring about a bullet in his head. Using extreme caution, he powered up Item 101 in the same way he'd done earlier that morning.

The spectators overlooking the process were in a state of complete awe, their jaws dropping.

After the plutonium was in place, Professor Alberstein clasped his hands together and observed how the powered nucleus capsule suddenly shot up into the sky. He quickly took charge of the mainframe and started twisting the knobs to control the capsule's flight path...

CHAPTER 8
LIVING A DAY IN A UTOPIAN PARADISE.

The first rays of sun breaking through the clouds splendidly complimented the chirrups of birds in a crisp morning breeze.

'ALL HAIL OUR ALMIGHTY SUPREME LEADER,' the eager masses cried out, falling to their knees.

The scores of people attending the rally were all draped in either ruby red or lily white gowns. They were from multicultural backgrounds, a melting pot of ethnicity. Everyone looked around with familiarity of the person that stood beside them. They seemed to be completely in their elements. These people were all facing a man who was standing on a large raised hydraulic raiser podium, dressed in a militaristic outfit. He stared down at his followers and said charismatically, 'Good morning, my children. Please stand near someone you haven't met before, that's now your place for the rest of annum. Now, rise for the start of our ceremony. '

As they stood up in unison it became evident that they were forming a peculiar pattern that could only be seen if one viewed them from above. From such a vantage point one would also be able to notice that the lettering on their gowns all read the same: Equality, Inclusivity, Diversity. Underneath the writing appeared an unsophisticated illustration of faceless people holding hands.

Once everybody was in an upright position, flares began to explode around them, creating vertical streams of red and white smoke that decorated the morning sky into a pretty postcard. Then a series of thundering fireworks followed, painting the picture into an even more beautiful scene of fiery red and white blooms.

'Every day is a blessing to us!' the leader called out over the crackling noise. 'We celebrate being alive!'

His followers watched with intent as their flag rose up from the bottom of a gigantic pole. When the flag was in position, all the way to the apex of the pole, everybody went silent and saluted in respect.

The leader then spread his arms and said, 'Like every day, we shall now recite the sacred maxim we live by.'

Growing in excitement, the crowd's faces rapidly turned from serious to jovial.

Shouting at the top of his voice, the leader stated, 'We work to live!'

To which the masses responded, 'We live to work!'

'Again,' he instructed.

'We live to work!' the crowd chorused.

Once the chanting and celebrations had been completed, the people in the crowd began to make their way out of the stadium, all trying to leave at once. Whilst walking to the nearest exit, Jayden Carter smiled at the stranger he stood with at the morning rally. He went by the name of Steven Leviki.

Leviki introduced himself and then said, 'It sure was a great rally this morning.'

'Yeah,' Jayden agreed, 'just like every morning to be perfectly honest.'

Steven chuckled. 'You can say that again.'

Radiating with energy, Jayden said, 'I feel so motivated to start my work day!'

'You're telling me,' replied Steven. 'I can't wait to get into my office.'

'Have a good one!' Jayden told his new acquaintance when they'd reached the exit.

'You too,' Steven responded before they headed to their respective jobs...

Jayden Carter arrived at the modern and ostentatious local hospital where he worked with a hearty smile. Beyond the large fleet of brand new ambulances in the parking lot he observed how a team of paramedics was busy wheeling a patient in on a mobile-bed into the emergency room.

A minute later he reached the hospital entrance with its automatic glass sliding doors and the sign that announced *Staff Only.* Jayden scanned his access key card over the digital scanner beneath the sign and a robotic female voice greeted him with the words, 'Access granted.'

'Top of the morning, Suzi!' he enthusiastically said to the receptionist as he walked past.

'Good morning to you too, Dr Carter,' she replied, fluttering her eyelids.

Ready to start the day, Jayden entered the men's restroom where he changed into his scrubs by putting on his surgical gown, face mask and bouffant cap. Finally, to complete his outfit, he pulled on his latex gloves. After stowing his wallet in his locker he confidently strolled out of the restroom, still smiling brightly.

Just as he was casually approaching the wards he monitored, a nurse ran up to Jayden and said 'Dr Carter, you must hurry! One of your patients have gone into cardiac arrest.'

'Oh dear!' he responded, wavering with genuine concern.

The nurse grabbed his forearm while saying, 'It was confirmed by Dr Flomist. He told us that the patient is quickly deteriorating. We're going to need you in the operating theatre over the next four to five hours to perform surgery. Otherwise the patient might not survive.'

'Not on my watch,' Jayden said loudly, quickening his steps. 'Time is of the essence.' He was now moving in a kind of serene purposefulness, striding along the magnolia corridor with its white slate flooring.

The surgery room was devoid of beauty. Jayden Carter stared at the sedated patient where he lay in isolated silence, so peaceful and unaware of the dangers his body was facing. It was rather cool inside and the sharp smell of disinfectant hung in the air.

Touching the patient's fragile rupturing skin, Dr Carter began the operating procedure. His posture was remarkably upright and every action he took was intricate and sophisticated. As he was making progress, his mood changed from cheerful to serious. He barked commands at colleagues as he dictated the course of the complex surgery.

'We're losing him!' one of the nurses shrieked when a continuous high-pitched beep came from the electronic heart monitor machine.

This didn't distract Jayden, not by any stretch of the imagination. He used his sharp surgical tools to work efficiently and with absolute precision. The nurses surrounding him were in total awe of his expertise. While performing the procedure, droplets of sweat intermittently trickled down his freckled face and his eyebrows were permanently raised (brought on by his intense concentration), exposing the lines and veins across his forehead. When he was done with his work, he looked up and smiled.

The heartbeat monitor started beeping in rhythmic pulses and the nurses began to give him a round of applause. Jayden joined in the applause, humbly thanking his helpful staff as he did so. A saved life had somehow injected beauty back into the room.

After the successful operation, Jayden was walking to the accident and emergency department when he noticed a warning sign that read *Caution, Wet Floor* in the hallway. Here was a woman wearing a t-shirt, baggy joggers and a pair of trainers. Beside her was a bucket filled with soapy water.

'Hi, we haven't yet met each other,' Jayden said. 'I'm Dr Carter.'

'I'm Brenda, one of the cleaners,' she replied, leaning on the mop she was holding. 'Nice to meet you, Dr Carter.'

'Brenda, let me just say: great work today! I want to thank you so much for your service to our esteemed hospital. The place wouldn't be the same without you performing your job so well.'

Brenda blushed and then changed the subject. 'I've actually heard a lot about you, Dr Carter. The staff here all say you are brilliant. They tell me you've saved so many lives.'

'I respect the sanctity of every patient. No one is supposed to be another statistic. My patients are me, love keeps us alive and we can survive anything if we care.'

'That is so inspiring' she responded, touching her heart with her free hand.

'You inspire me more, Brenda. The work you do is outstanding. We all know that cleanliness is a hospital's most important priority.'

'Thank you so much, Dr Carter, it feels good to be acknowledged.'

When Jayden Carter arrived home from work that afternoon, the sun had sunk low into the sky and the remaining twilight was swiftly fading away. A velvet blanket of night sky would soon replace the golden day. It had been a long day for Jayden, not only because of the surgery he'd performed, but he'd also had to deal with a number of patients, suffering from various degrees of illness.

Turning his keys and opening the front door, he called, 'Good evening, my beautiful family!'

His wife greeted from the kitchen while his young son met him in the doorway. Jayden smiled as he looked at the boy lovingly. 'Dylan, how was school today, little buddy?' he asked.

'Daddy, I need to tell you something,' Dylan responded with a nervous grin on his face.

'What is it, son?' Jayden said in a gentle voice. 'You know you can tell me anything.'

Young Dylan was gazing at the ground, but both parents noticed his cheeky smirk as he said, 'Today, in school, we all had to talk about our role models. I told the rest of the class that my dad is mine.'

'That's very sweet, Dylan, my boy,' Jayden murmured, his heart bursting with pride. 'I can't tell you how much that means to me,' He knelt down, brought Dylan closer to him and embraced him in a hug.

'You inspire me,' Dylan continued his praise. 'When I'm older, I want to be just like you.'

Jayden stood upright and placed both his hands upon his son's shoulders. 'Well, Dylan, why do you think I inspire you so much?'

Shrugging his shoulders under his father's grip, Dylan said, 'I don't know, Dad, you just do.'

'I don't work for myself, I work for everyone around me,' Jayden now told his only boy. 'It's all for the betterment of our community, therefore we put the nation's interests before our own. We must yield if our interests contradict those of our leaders.'

'Wow,' Dylan replied, locking eyes with his dad.

Jayden Carter lowered his voice ever so slightly and then said, 'Son, as long as you follow the strict rules of our society, by dedicating your life to work then, one day, you'll be exactly like me.'

A tear rolled down little Dylan's cheek. He sniffled and jumped into his father's arms. Jayden caught him in the air and elevated him up to his shoulders. Dylan threw his arms above his head in excitement. Then his father began to pace around the house with the boy still on his shoulders. As they entered the kitchen, Sandra glanced at them and smiled the way only a loving mother could. That warm, melting smile that said, 'We are so fortunate to have each other.'

'Live to work, Dad.' Dylan said out of the blue.

Jayden carefully bent down and placed the boy back on the ground. Ruffling Dylan's hair, he proudly said, 'Work to live, son'.

After they had enjoyed supper, it was the end of a perfect day in paradise as the Carter family went to bed, excited for the next day to arrive.

CHAPTER 9
EARTH-SHAKE

It was a blissful night, so absolutely tranquil and quiet in the Carter home. Sandra and Jayden were fast asleep after putting Dylan to bed by singing him his favorite lullaby.

Just as Jayden's snores settled into a rhythmic pattern, he suddenly woke up and sat upright. At first he thought he'd had a night terror, but then he heard the echo of the sound. There was a loud thud coming from the backyard – BOOM! Jayden's eyes were now wide open in alertness.

'What's happening?' Sandra asked as she also heard the sound and started to feel the bed shaking beneath them. Then they heard a scream coming from Dylan's bedroom.

'It must be an earthquake,' Jayden guessed, biting his lower lip.

His words weren't cold when Dylan ran into the master bedroom. 'I'm scared, Mommy,' the boy moaned in a frightened voice.

Once he had lifted his son into their bed, Jayden said, 'I want the both of you to wait here while I go outside to investigate what is causing this commotion. Perhaps it's not an earthquake but something else altogether.' His wife and child nodded their heads in accord.

He got out of bed and donned his nightgown and slippers, then went downstairs and fetched a flashlight from the broom cupboard before opening the kitchen door leading to his spacious backyard. He wasn't prepared for what he saw next. There, in the centre of the lawn, was a massive gaping hole...

'Oh my soul!' Jayden cried out. His jaw dropped and he had to pinch himself and rub his eyes to make sure he wasn't sleepwalking in a dream. After remaining motionless for what seemed like an eternity - glaring at the hole in the ground in confusion - he eventually edged closer, tip-toeing towards the oval-shaped opening.

Meanwhile, back in the master bedroom, young Dylan was trembling with fear. His mother was cradling him, holding him tight against her chest. She kept on calming him down by saying things like 'Everything is fine, honey' and 'All will be okay, don't worry about Daddy.'

Peering over the side of the hole, Jayden used the flashlight to illuminate the surface at the bottom. As he did so, however, a bright green beam reflected back up to him, meeting the yellow glow of the flashlight in a kaleidoscope of dancing glimmers.

'Are my eyes deceiving me?' he asked himself, frowning.

He courageously manoeuvred himself down the hole and reached the bottom a few moments later. The object he found there was of course nothing else but Professor Alberstein's nucleus capsule! It was light in weight, so Jayden flipped it up onto the lawn surrounding the hole. When he'd climbed out, he stood there and studied the object with fascination. The smooth texture was something he'd never seen before. He cringed as he beamed the flashlight light over the nucleus. Then, as he cautiously knelt down and touched the pulsating shell, the green glow got weaker, almost disappearing completely. Now that he could clearly see the exterior of the object, Jayden Carter all of a sudden felt extremely nauseous. But he swallowed the bile in his throat and continued to investigate.

There was a flap on the side, which he opened to reveal a strange-looking lever. He tentatively pulled this lever and the device hissed open to uncover its interior. The tube that had once held the plutonium matter was now empty, although Jayden didn't know that the nuclear material had been in there in the first place. Shifting the empty tube to the side, he noticed tiny holes beyond a concoction of wires. These holes began to emit a resonance that sounded very much like static white noise. The sound kept on changing pitch, becoming higher and lower, changing in frequency as the seconds passed.

Back in the courtyard at Area 51, green lights also started flickering from the centre of the mainframe machine. This was accompanied by an ear-piercing hum, with an electrical current now running through the mainframe's antenna, as it circled around like a satellite in orbit.

'This is the moment we've all been waiting for, people!' Professor Alberstein called out.

Attached to the mainframe was a large studio microphone. The professor positioned his mouth in front of this microphone and said loudly, 'Come in. Come in.'

Hearing this sound, emerging from the nucleus over the static, Jayden quivered. 'Hello?' he said hesitantly.

'This is Professor Alberstein. I am a representative of Planet Earth. We come in peace.'

'Earth?' Jayden replied, raising an eyebrow. 'I've never heard of such a place. Who is this? Is this a joke?'

Upon hearing the stranger's voice at Area 51, everyone started cheering and celebrating the ground-breaking moment. 'We've done it!' Fisher shouted. 'Yes!' Earl followed.

'Quiet!' the president ordered them. 'Let me take over.' He approached the microphone and said, 'We are the human race and I am the president of the most powerful country on the planet.'

'Human? President? Country?' Jayden responded. 'I don't understand what you are saying.'

Professor Alberstein pulled the president away from the microphone by his arm and then angrily whispered, 'Mr President, stop, or I'll abort the mission.' The president's face went red but he somehow managed to keep his composure and allow Alberstein to intervene.

The professor spoke quietly into the microphone. 'Sorry for the confusion, my friend,' he said. 'We are inhabitants from another world.'

'Wow!' Jayden replied, all of a sudden thrilled instead of scared and baffled. 'So you are like aliens?'

'Exactly,' said the professor. 'Our world is probably vastly different from yours.'

'In what way?' Jayden asked. 'Do you live to work and work to live, like we do?'

'Work, for many, isn't really life in our society,' came the reply.

'Whoa!' Jayden Carter now shouted, stunned by the concept.

'Yes, as humans, we operate a *capitalist* system, we only work for our desired wage in order to pay for entertainment… You see, we pursue the arts, my friend.'

Jayden leaned closer to the nucleus capsule. 'What are these *arts* you speak of? he inquired.

Professor Alberstein proceeded to explain exactly what humans enjoyed as their hobbies, including books, films, music, stage performances and other more traditional forms of art such as paintings and sculptures in museums and at exhibitions.

On the one hand Jayden was in awe and on the other hand he was confused. 'BLASPHEMY,' he shouted as he rushed to his garden shed where he fetched a shovel and buried Item 101, the exceptionally sophisticated alien communication device.

CHAPTER 10
SECRET'S OUT?

Jayden was in a state of sheer panic, fuelled by the adrenaline pumping through his veins.

Throwing the shovel aside, he wiped a mixture of sweat and tears from his cheeks with the sleeve of his pyjama shirt. He then took a deep breath of air – in through his nose and out through his mouth – while closing his eyes for a moment to gather his thoughts. When he was ready, he went back into the house and returned to the bedroom upstairs where his Sandra was still busy calming Dylan down.

As soon as he entered the room, she looked at him expectantly while saying, 'Well?'

Speaking very calmly and articulately, Jayden replied with, 'It's really nothing to worry about, darling. It was just a mild tremor... kind of what I suspected, to tell you the truth.'

His wife didn't say anything in return. Instead, she heaved a heavy sigh of relief.

'What's a tremor, Mummy?' Dylan asked. Struggling with the 'r' sound, he pronounced it as *tlemul*.

'Don't worry, son,' Sandra assured him. 'A tremor is merely a fancy word for a minor earthquake. They happen all the time here where we live.'

Dylan smiled, also relieved that the scary moment had passed. Jayden took his hand and said, 'I think it's time for you to go back to bed now, little one. You need to rest well. You have school in the morning.'

'Okay, Daddy,' Dylan replied, still smiling timidly.

'Good boy,' Jayden said, helping his son off the bed and escorting him to the door in a hurry. Once Dylan was out in the corridor, Jayden slammed the door shut. Sandra looked at him in pure bewilderment.

'Wait, Daddy…' Dylan moaned from the other side of the door.

'What is it now?' Jayden shouted in frustration. His wife glared him down in disgust.

'Work to live, Daddy,' Dylan quietly chanted.

Jayden glanced at the door, feeling both ashamed and disorientated. After snapping back into reality seconds later, he quickly shook his head. 'Uhm, yes, live to work, son,' he said slowly and reluctantly.

Dylan said goodnight and as soon as they could hear his footsteps away from the door, Sandra asked, 'What's wrong, Jayden?'

'Nothing!' he snapped. There was an uncontrollable and sinister loudness in his voice as he gazed at her with murky eyes.

She met his gaze and muttered, 'All right then. Let's go back to sleep.'

As Jayden switched off the bedside lamp, he sank into the mattress and buried his head in his pillow.

What would usually be a smooth transition into a dream, now became a burden. His mind was swimming with dozens of thoughts while he tossed and turned in the bed, grappling with the darkness - a new kind of darkness that felt as if it was consuming him. He soon realised that he was panting heavily, trying to catch his breath. Holding the pillow over his ears, Jayden attempted to block out that piercing white noise and the eerie voice from the radio transmission earlier. The sounds seemed to be continuously looping around in his head: *Earth, Humans, President....* Although exhausted, Jayden couldn't sleep for hours. The experience in the backyard kept on haunting him and he, in turn, kept on pushing the thoughts away. 'Should I do it? He asked himself as he forced his eyes closed. Persistence finally led to a shut-down, then dream state ensued, allowing his body and mind to be refuelled.

CHAPTER 11
A LIVING NIGHTMARE?

'My children, as one we are flawed and weak,' a man shouted from the rooftops, using a red megaphone. 'But together we have the power to rise up. Together we can achieve anything!'

The masses below showed their respect and obedience by cheering loudly, almost hysterically. The man was seemingly the supreme leader but his followers couldn't see his face; it was hidden behind a military-style helmet that was two sizes too big, causing it to hang loosely over his eyes. Unlike the signature white robes the masses were wearing, he was dressed in a neatly pressed army uniform.

'Strip yourselves of the chains holding you apart from one another!' the leader continued, his voice echoing across the square. 'Let yourselves free!'

In the centre of the crowd a bonfire was burning brightly, sending sparks and twirling smoke into the air. Upon hearing the instruction to become free, all the people in the square promptly removed their gowns and hurled them onto the fire, creating the sweet smell of melting cotton.

'Let us rebel against oppression!' he shouted into the megaphone. 'Let us make our voices heard and end this once and for all! Repeat after me: No more suppression! No more oppression! No more repression!'

The people began to recite the words while marching in a circle around the bonfire. Their chosen leader watched the spectacle unfold, still shouting. 'Let us unleash ourselves from the shackled despotism! We have been brainwashed! Our current so-called utopian government represents nothing more than a tyrannical reign. They've been hiding the truth from us and now, children, join me. It is time for a revolution!'

A man in the crowd climbed onto the square's main attraction – a marble statue of the previously elected leader. Other people helped him to tie several lengths of rope around it and (once he was back on the ground) they pulled with all their might, causing the statue to topple over. It landed on the concrete surface of the square with a massive crackle and shattered to pieces.

The man who had brought the rope picked up the statue's head and approached the new leader, holding it high above his head.'

'Yes!' the leader cried out. 'Your current supreme leader is no more; his reign is finally over. Welcome to a free new word!'

In the distance, coming towards them from down a hill, was an army of uniformed government officials. They were heavily armed and the labels on their vests said RIOT MILITARY POLICE. Other than their automatic weapons they also carried riot gear such as tear gas and shields to try and disband the protest.

'We won't back down,' the leader said loudly, glaring at the police soldiers who were approaching rapidly. From the other side of the square a fleet of military tanks came up the hill and above them fighter planes began to fill the skies. The people on the ground started pushing and shoving to get away from the attack.

Then all hell broke loose.

The shots came down onto them like a torrential rain shower, pelting down relentlessly. This bullet storm was accompanied by a blizzard of fire arrows that rasped and sizzled through the air. A medley of flames lit up the sky and wavy ribbons of light shone down in chrysalis-brightness. The brutal attack was enough to send chills down spines and make hearts hammer in chest cavities. From the square came blood-curdling screams, deathly cries of agony as the fracturing and rupturing arsenal of tracer bullets, fire arrows, thunder tubes and teargas cans struck with terrific force. The hazy air was now tinted in a mist of a lava-red spray, while a nauseating waft of magma mixed with volcanic ash arose. The scene was that of an obliterating massacre; a gush of collateral carnage; a choreographed dance of decapitation.

After the slaughtering, a cold and malevolent wind circulated around the bloodbath in the square. It could be described as a wind of despair, a wind that quietly howled.

The new supreme leader walked through what was left behind – the carcasses of all the people who had applauded and praised him so energetically earlier. The carnage now almost appeared to be apocalyptic in nature. Coming to a standstill beside the fallen statue, he straightened his military uniform while staring at the dead with tears of guilt, regret and pain filling his eyes. Then he lifted his right arm and saw a splatter of thick red liquid in the palm of his hand. 'Who am I? he whispered to himself. After a long moment of introspection he asked, 'What have I become?'

In the morning, Jayden's alarm went off with a bang. This surprised him since he usually awoke long before the time the alarm was set for, peacefully and slowly, not in shock and horror. Looking at his right palm, he noticed that it was clean and he gave a sigh of relief.

He shook the sleep from his head, then yanked himself upright and said loudly, 'I can't do it.'

'Can't do what?' Sandra asked in a slight panic. 'What's going on, Jayden?'

Jayden rolled over and laid on his stomach. He covered his head with his pillow.

CHAPTER 12
EFFICIENCY AWARDS

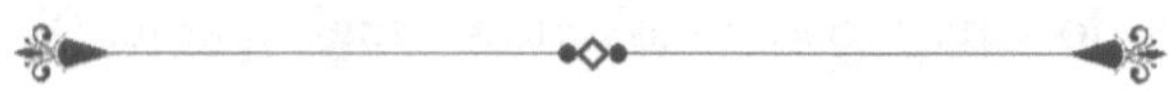

'I've absolutely had it with you!' Sandra told Jayden, wagging her finger at him. In his state of consternation he only made an indistinguishable muttering noise in return.

'Look at me,' Sandra pleaded. Jayden rolled over reluctantly and held his wife's gaze, still not saying a word.

'The annual efficiency awards ceremony is starting soon,' she told him. 'Are you going to get up?'

'Fine,' Jayden eventually replied. He sluggishly dragged his legs out of bed and placed his feet onto the floor. Then a frown formed on his face when he added, 'What's the point?'

'The point is to acknowledge our neighbours and all the other individuals around us who work so hard to make this society productive,' she reminded him.

He rolled his eyes and responded by saying, 'No, not that. I mean, what's the point of life, Sandra?'

She looked back at him in bemusement. 'I don't know what has gotten into you, but whatever it is, we'll figure it out together. I love you and I'm here for you. But for now, you have to get dressed and go to the efficiency awards. The government has arranged a beautiful ceremony and attendance is mandatory.'

Jayden pushed himself to his feet while saying, 'You don't understand. You'll never understand.' Then, without changing into daywear or brushing his teeth, he went downstairs and out into the driveway to start his car's engine...

★★★

'Live to work!' the supreme leader announced.

'Work to live!' the masses replied in a chorus.

'Welcome all!' the supreme leader then said with a hearty smile on his face. He paused while his followers applauded. Once the cheers had died down, he said, 'Ladies and gentleman, I'd like to thank each and every one of the council members who made this ceremony possible.' Another round of clapping followed.

The supreme leader uncovered a table stacked with golden trophies, each of them engraved with a name. 'Before we reward everyone in our society for being such hard workers, I want to ask a random member in the audience - one of our model citizens, if you like - to come to the podium and say a few words.' He closed his eyes and pointed. 'You,' he commanded when his finger suddenly stopped at an arbitrary location.

'Me?' Jayden Carter said in surprise. Everybody was now staring at him and his face flushed as he became self-conscious of his faded nightgown and battered slippers.

'Yes, you,' the supreme leader said, opening his eyes and throwing his hands in the air.

Steven Leviki, the gentleman Jayden had met the day before, patted him on the back to encourage him. Jayden, emotionless, slowly dragged himself across the square while the others applauded excitedly. Before he knew it, he was behind the microphone on the podium, all eyes fixed on his tired body.

The supreme leader put a comforting hand on his shoulder and Jayden looked around as the audience before him turned into a fuzzy blur. Every second that ticked over felt like a million years, as a countless number of thoughts raced into his head at once. He turned to behold the supreme leader and then began to tremble.

Clenching his jaw and balling his fists, Jayden approached the microphone. As he leaned forward to adjust its height, all he could see in his mind's eye was the image of blood spatter in the palm of his hand.

'First of all,' he said lethargically, 'thank you so much for this honour.' The crowd once again erupted in a loud applause. 'Just keep on living to work,' Jayden declared, his lips nearly touching the microphone.

'Work to live!' the masses shouted.

As quickly as he could, Jayden then stepped off the podium. While returning to his place in the audience, he was short of breath and his heart was beating like a jackhammer against his ribcage.

Steven Leviki stared at him. 'What was that?' he asked. On the podium, the supreme leader started calling out names and handing out trophies.

Jayden turned his back on Steven, refusing to reply. Steven tapped him on the shoulder but Jayden continued to ignore him. After a long moment of gazing into the sky, Jayden forced a smile (his first smile of the day, in fact) and said, 'Listen, Steven, I need to tell you something.'

'I'm sorry,' replied Steven Leviki, looking the other way, 'there's nothing for us to discuss.'

'No,' Jayden said loudly, 'I mean, you don't understand. I have something to tell you. It's very important. It's something that threatens our entire society.'

Upon hearing the word 'threatens' Steven's demeanor changed instantly. 'What is wrong, my friend?' he now asked, genuinely concerned. 'You know you can always count on talking to me. We're almost like brothers, you know?'

Jayden cringed as he looked at the man, noticing the sincerity in his eyes. He embraced Steven and began to sob uncontrollably. Steven Leviki had a perplexed expression on his face, but returned the hug all the same.

After a short while Jayden stood back, then retrieved a scrap of paper and a fountain pen from the pocket of his nightgown and proceeded to write something down. He handed the note to Steven whilst saying, 'Make your way to this address shortly after we depart from here.'

CHAPTER 13
BUSINESS MEETING

After returning home from the efficiency awards ceremony, Jayden went into the kitchen with his wife and said, 'Won't you take a seat, honey?'

Sandra sat down and looked up at her husband in curiosity. Outside, the clouds were gathering and they both knew a storm was approaching.

Following a prolonged moment of silence, Jayden broke the ice by saying, 'I've decided to come clean.'

'Please do,' she replied, furrowing her brow.

'I know I've been acting... well... different lately. And it's about time I tell you what's on my mind.'

'Yes! Please do,' Sandra repeated, raising her voice to express her seriousness.

Jayden gave her a soul-piercing stare and then said sadly, 'One of my patients… uhm… let's just say that he didn't make it.'

'Oh, I'm so sorry,' his beloved wife said in her best effort to make him feel better.

Looking the other way, Jayden buried his face in his hands and began to cry. 'I'm finding it really hard to talk about these kinds of things,' he said in-between sobs.

'I completely understand, darling,' she responded. 'I'm so sorry I've pressed you like that. I honestly had no idea, but now I understand why you've been acting strangely.'

Jayden stopped crying and looked down to hide the twinkle in his eyes. 'It's a very traumatising experience for me,' he now said. 'And that's why I've hired a therapist to come over the house to… uhm… you know, to help me get over the mental scars.'

'Please, say no more, love,' Sandra replied in comprehension. Then she glanced at the staircase through the kitchen door and added, 'I believe Dylan is playing in his room. I'll go and fetch him and we'll go out for a walk so you can have all the privacy you need.'

'Thank you so much, Sandra. You really are the best wife in the world. Don't you ever forget that.'

She stood up and touched his shoulder before walking out of the kitchen. As she reached the doorway, she turned and tilted her head to the side. 'Live to work,' she said, smiling lovingly.

'Work to live,' Jayden responded with a wide grin on his face. But, as soon as Sandra went up the stairs, the grin was replaced by an expression that spelled anger and distress.

Sandra and Dylan came down a minute later and she said, 'Good luck! Give me a call when you're done, will you?' Jayden promised that he would, whereafter his wife and son left the house.

Shortly after that, there was a knock at the door. 'Open up neighbour, it's me,' a muffled voice sounded from the outside.

Jayden answered the door and Steven Leviki hugged him as he entered. 'Good afternoon, my brother,' he said sincerely. 'Thank you for inviting me to your luxurious abode.'

'No problem,' Jayden replied. There was a hint of nervous undertone in his voice. Staring at Steven where he was standing in the doorway, he contemplated for a while. He studied Steven's face and observed something that could only be described as a lust for life. And in that moment, Jayden Carter thought, *I see my previous life in those eyes. I'd do anything to get it back.*

CHAPTER 14
SECRETS REVEALED

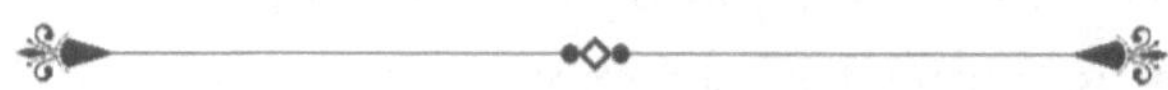

'Please sit down,' Jayden said, pointing at an overstuffed brown sofa in the living room. He felt miserable, yet his face expressed no emotion. Steven, however, had the complete opposite emotional appearance as he sat down with a big grin playing across his lips.

'What's with the spring in your step?' Jayden asked judgingly.

'I don't know what you mean,' replied Steven, glowing with a natural level of energy. 'I'm always like this. Life is a blessing and we should embrace it.'

Taking a seat on a leather ottoman beside the sofa, Jayden pressed his fingertips together and sighed. *This is going to be harder than I anticipated,* he thought to himself.

Steven Leviki looked at him, still wearing that wide grin, ignoring Jayden's negativity. 'If we could, let's try and make this quick,' he said in his most polite tone of voice.

'Are you in a rush?' asked Jayden, arching his eyebrows.

'I'm meant to be in the office right now, Jayden. Actually, the entire team is depending on me to be there.'

Jayden gave a sarcastic chuckle. 'Don't you just make the coffee for all the other important ones?' he asked, already knowing the answer.

Steven's friendly face turned sombre. 'Look, I am a valuable cog in a much bigger corporate machine,' he said defensively, raising a finger to accentuate his point.

'Of course you are,' Jayden replied cynically. They both smiled, although one was a sincere smile whilst the other one was forced and fake. 'All right then,' Jayden said after an uncomfortable moment of silence. Then he lowered his voice to barely above a whisper. 'You might want to clear your schedule for the day, Steven. What I'm about to tell you, uhm... I guess it will... will most likely hit you like a ton of bricks.' He was trying to sound confident but he kept on stumbling on his words. Deep down it felt as if his blood was starting to boil. Looking at his previously steady hands, he saw that they were now trembling with nervousness.

Steven Leviki noticed this sudden mood change but he kept his cool. He wasn't nervous at all. If anything, he was intrigued and kind of excited. While squinting against the natural light coming from the window to his right, he asked, 'Why are you whispering like that, hmm?'

'Keep your voice down!' Jayden pleaded, much louder than before. He glared out the window and added, 'We don't know who's listening.'

Once Steven had nodded to indicate that he understood, Jayden Carter began to tell him about his traumatic experience with Item 101 out in the backyard. It took him the better part of fifteen minutes.

'You've got to be kidding me!' Steven said after hearing the somewhat unbelievable story.

Jayden gave another heavy sigh. 'Believe me, I wish I was.'

'You know it's illegal to spread false information about our regime, right?'

'I'm telling you it's true!' Jayden shouted, banging a fist on the coffee table.

Rising to his feet, Steven Leviki approached Jayden and placed a gentle hand on his shoulder. 'Relax, my friend,' he said quietly. 'Everything is going to be fine.' Upon witnessing Jayden's confused state, he said, 'I'm no expert, but this sounds a lot like a mild case of tactile hallucinations to me.'

Even though his visitor's words and actions came across as sympathetic, Jayden buried his face in his hands as he started to hyperventilate in anxiety. Before he could say anything else, Steven spoke again. 'You know what, Jayden? I'm only saying this because you're like a bother to me. I really think we should find some therapy for you. I'll help you through this and guide you every step of the way.'

At this point, Jayden angrily pushed Steven's hand away from his shoulder. 'I give up,' he muttered.

'I'm going to call someone from the government who might be able to help you,' Steven said, wandering over to the telephone in the corner of the room. Once he had reached the communication device, he picked up the handset and began to dial a number.

When he observed what Steven was doing, Jayden flew from his chair and ran towards him. Steven Leviki first looked at him in shock, then closed his eyes and clenched his stomach muscles, preparing his body for the impact. In a fast diving movement, Jaden propelled himself into Steven's torso, knocking him to the ground in the process. The force of the impact sent the telephone soaring through the air, unplugging it from the wall socket. It landed on the carpet, eight feet away.

With both of them now on the floor, a struggle ensued, Jayden on top in an effort to control the situation. He grabbed Steven's arms where he lay flat on his back. Steven wriggled around under his attacker's weight while Jayden begged in a loud voice, 'Please, just let me prove it to you!'

'You're crazy,' Steven hissed through his teeth. Then, as he continued to struggle under Jayden's firm grip, he belted out, 'Help! Somebody, please help! I'm being assaulted!' Suddenly, by using the swinging motion of his legs, he managed to shove Jayden's body off his chest. He squirmed away and pushed himself to his feet as fast as possible. Rushing to the front door, he began to fiddle with the handle. 'How do you unlock this thing?' he cried out in despair.

Like a wild animal chasing down its prey, Jayden Carter raced towards Steven while he was still struggling to unlock the door. Taking advantage of the situation, Jayden covered Steven's nose and mouth with one hand whilst gripping his body with the other arm.

★★★

Steven's wife, Vanessa, was in her living room, working as a babysitter by looking after a bunch of young children when the telephone suddenly rang; something quite unusual for this time of the day.

She scurried to the phone and pickedt up. 'Hello?' she said.

'Good day, ma'am,' replied a male voice. 'May I speak to Steven Leviki please?'

'Hi, this is his wife, Vanessa. I really do apologise. He's currently at the office. Can I perhaps take a message?'

'Hello Vanessa,' said the man on the other side of the line. 'That's rather strange. I'm Sam from his office and I was actually calling to ask if he's coming into work today.'

'What?' Vanessa exclaimed. 'That's very worrying!'

'Well, when you see him again,' replied Sam, 'please remind him that attendance at work is mandatory. It's against the law of the supreme leader to take a day off without permission.'

Vanessa shook her head as if he was able to see her. 'I don't know what to say,' she told him. 'I'll find out what's happening and keep you informed.' Then she said goodbye and hung up.

★★★

Steven Leviki awoke in a daze. 'It was all a dream,' he said to himself with his eyes still half closed.

Shaking his head, he slowly returned back to a state of consciousness and then realised the disturbing reality, upon noticing that he wasn't in his bed. While peering around and recognising the familiar surroundings of Jayden's living room, the upsetting memory of the attack came rushing back. His immediate reaction was to scream, but his attempt failed since his mouth was gagged by something that felt like duct tape. Looking down, Steven saw that he was bound to a wooden chair, his wrists and ankles tied tightly to its armrests and legs with thick rope. He tried to kick and rip himself free, to no avail.

There was a cold chill in the house and he began to shiver; not only from the chill, but also in fear. Tears started rolling down his cheeks. Flashes of Steven's work and family life were swimming around in his head. Straining to control his thoughts, he scanned the room to see if anything in there could help him escape. There was absolutely nothing. He was stuck. Captured. Like a prisoner.

Jayden walked back into the living room, carrying a dirty shovel in gloved hands. Steven's stomach churned. 'Don't kill me!' he tried to shout, but the only sound that came from underneath the strip of duct tape was a muffled groan.

'Wait here,' Jayden ordered as he disappeared into the kitchen. He returned moments later, now holding the mud-covered nucleus from Item 101. Steven was shocked and flabbergasted, even more so than when he'd seen Jayden with the shovel earlier. Realising that the object was extra-terrestrial, Steven Leviki was scared to death at first. But, as with so many others who'd seen Item 101 before him, his face quickly turned into a gaze of awe.

Jayden set the nucleus down on the mantelpiece above the fireplace, then walked over to Steven and pulled the duct tape from his mouth in a swift motion. 'Ouch!' Steven moaned.

'Now do you believe me?' Jayden asked with a sneer. He motioned in the direction of the nucleus with his chin. 'We've been brainwashed, Steven,' he said. 'The government has been hiding this secret from us our entire lives. It's oppression and an imposition on our freedom.'

When Steven didn't respond, Jayden went into the kitchen and came back with a sharp carving knife. Once again, the visitor shuddered, fearing for his life. 'Relax,' Jayden told him, cutting the ropes from his wrists and ankles.

'Thank you so much,' Steven replied once he was free to move again.

'Look down at your hands,' Jayden instructed. 'They are clean. I want you to keep it that way.' Then he touched Steven's arm and asked, 'Do you want to take a closer look at that nucleus now?'

'Perhaps tomorrow,' Steven said in return. 'This has been quite an exhausting experience for me. Right now, all I want to do is go home and get some rest, if you don't mind.'

Jayden smiled while reaching into his pocket and producing a business card. 'Okay,' he said softly. He handed the card to Steven. 'Here is my phone number. Give me a call once you've slept on it.'

'Will do,' Steven replied, still visibly shaken up. He proceeded to put the paper in his coat pocket and left into the night.

CHAPTER 15
THE LEVIKIS

It was a snowy and gloomy evening when Steven Leviki sprinted through the streets in order to escape the freezing cold air. Although the neighbourhood was well illuminated by the bright yellow light of street lamps, he still made sure to watch his step, avoiding the slippery edges of the frosty sidewalk.

While pausing to catch his breath at one of the many intersections, Steven looked up at the glow of a silvery moon, surrounded by a bright blanket of stars. Nature normally enthralled him, but now it fuelled a sense of anxiety instead. He began to shiver, not sure if it was because of his nerves or the chill in the atmosphere. As a result, he started panicking even more and picked up his pace. His home wasn't far now.

***

Back at the Leviki house, Vanessa was pacing around in the kitchen, her mind a whirlpool of thoughts racing around in circles. She was worried sick about her husband. Her fists were involuntarily clenched as she held them firmly to her sides. Drops of perspiration were trickling down from her forehead and into her eyes. With every second of the clock ticking over, her anxiety intensified. *Where is he?* she kept on repeating to herself in her head.

★★★

There was a lump in Steven's throat when he finally reached his house. He stared at the brass keyhole in the front door while patting his empty pockets, realising that he had left his keys in the ceramic bowl on the dining room table. He reluctantly extended his index finger towards the doorbell, but then thought, *What if Vanessa is sleeping? I don't want to wake her.*

With legs feeling like jelly, he staggered backwards and collapsed to the ground in an emotional meltdown. He first cradled himself into a ball, weeping quietly, then propped himself up on his hands and knees and shouted, 'Why?' While snowflakes caressed his cheeks he repeated the word, this time in a whisper: 'Why?'

Vanessa heard the commotion outside and slowly unlocked the front door from the inside. Upon peeking out and noticing the figure on the snow-covered lawn she gave a high-pitched shriek. Steven looked up at her and when she saw who it was she said, 'Oh, honey, it's you. Where on earth have you been?'

Steven grinned foolishly, then replied in a shaky voice, 'I was just performing my civic duties, love. I locked myself out and it's mighty cold out here, believe me.'

'Oh, you poor thing,' Vanessa murmured while helping him to his feet. She embraced him and said, 'Come inside, you're freezing.' They went into the comfort of their home, Vanessa locking the door behind them and Steven rubbing his hands together against the cold. He was shaking like a leaf. 'Let's get you into bed,' Vanessa whispered. 'You've got another big day at work tomorrow.'

Even though the interior of their modest house was warm, the bedroom somehow felt colder. Steven Leviki was still shivering, so he pulled the blankets all the way up to his chin as he closed his eyes, thinking about happier family times in the past - the day he'd met Vanessa, their wedding ceremony, and the birth of their children. They've had so much fun over the years... These memories were vivid at first and then gradually became foggy and hazy. The pleasant dream was sadly fading away from him. It was soon replaced by the disgusting image of the shiny green and turquoise shape of the alien nucleus Jayden had shown him. The more Steven tried to escape from this new nightmare, the more it haunted him; relentlessly looping, causing a constant pounding in his chest. Outside, it had stopped snowing and the moon had become even brighter, but the world appeared to be lifeless, devoid of hope, a creeping sorrow.

★★★

The cast in their costumes bowed and then the curtains closed with a swoosh. The crowd erupted in loud applause, whistling and clapping hands in appreciation. Steven Leviki had a front-row seat. He was dressed in a formal white shirt, a black tuxedo and a maroon bow tie. Sheer happiness was burning inside him and reflected on his face. His smile was a flair of joy. His energy was unparalleled, like that of a lightning strike.

★★★

Steven's mood changed instantly, with the image of a holographic flash of light shooting into his soul, as he woke up in the middle of the night. The happy memories came flooding back, only now they were a little bit different. They were better.

With beams of delight dancing through his thoughts, he shut his eyes and fell asleep again in a heartbeat.

★★★

A group of people reeking of old sweat and burnt coal walked around in the city. They were all wearing torn rags and their heads were shaved, exposing lumps and old scars. Their nails were long and dirty. The ground beneath their ruptured feet was a perfect mixture of sand and mud. This was the urban part of the city and it was highly populated. Everywhere you looked there were people in sight. The houses were derelict, mostly built out of scrap metal, cardboard, tin and acrylic sheets; weak structures that could be blown to pieces by the wind of only the slightest storm. Coloured items of clothing hung from askew rooftops, faded over the years by the harsh weather. Many of the people balanced clay jugs on their heads. The non-functional sewer system released a foul, sour odour. A man with a gaping wound on his thigh drank brown water from a plastic container. A family shared a small bowl of stale rice.

Steven Leviki was met by a group of young children with tears pouring down their cheeks.

'Welcome to our slum,' the boy in front greeted with a stutter.

'Why are you crying?' Steven asked, baffled.

'The people on the western outskirts of the city… they, uhm… they enjoy their arts, but it's at our expense.'

'What do you mean?'

'This is how so many of us live, because of the rules in our society. They need losers to have winners.'

★★★

Steven opened his eyes. They gradually widened as he returned to a lucid state. He was about to jump up when he contained himself, suddenly aware of the sleeping Vanessa beside him. After climbing out of bed as quietly as he could, he got dressed before tiptoeing down the stairs. What he didn't know was that his wife was already awake and that she was curiously peeking at him through an eyelid.

As soon as he'd left the house, Vanessa grabbed her coat and a pair of binoculars and went after him.

CHAPTER 16
MEET ME AROUND THE BACK

When Steven Leviki walked out of his house it was still dark outside, with daybreak an hour and a half away.

He began to make his way to Jayden's house on foot, wearing his thick winter coat over his woollen jersey and cotton shirt. A freezing breeze was blowing and his hands were red and numb. Steven started shivering and rubbed his hands together to generate friction (and subsequently heat, of course) while increasing his pace to a slow jog. Once the life had returned to his hands, he put them in his pockets and felt a folded piece of hard paper in one of them. Taking it out, he unfolded it and saw that it was the business card Jayden Carter had given him earlier.

'Don't need that anymore,' he muttered to himself. Glancing down at his wristwatch, he thought, *If I start running now, I could be at Jayden's place within fifteen minutes.* He tossed the business card into the gutter and began to run.

Behind him Vanessa was watching his every move, struggling to keep up with him. Which wasn't necessarily a bad thing, since she would have drawn Steven's attention if she got too close. She lifted the binoculars to her eyes just in time to see her husband drop the business card to the ground. After giving a loud sigh of aggravation, she decided to let him continue on his own whilst she would go after the business card. When she reached it, she picked it up and upon reading Jayden Carter's phone number and other personal details, she whispered, 'Perfect.' Her voice sounded almost evil. Vanessa Leviki turned back and headed in the opposite direction.

★★★

A loud banging on the front door awoke Jayden, Sandra and Dylan Carter.

'Who could that possibly be?' Sandra asked as she jolted upright, noticing that the sun had risen yet.

'You check on Dylan,' Jayden told her. 'Let me deal with whoever that is.'

'Wait!' Sandra called as her husband jumped out of bed and hurried down the stairs.

He answered the door twenty seconds later and said quietly, 'Steven, go around the back, I'll meet you there in an hour.' Before Steven could object, Jayden closed the door in his face.

Going back upstairs, Jayden found Dylan standing outside his room in the hallway. 'Who was that, Daddy?' Dylan asked, rubbing the sleep from his eyes with his tiny fists. Sandra now emerged from her son's room and looked at her husband expectantly.

Jayden regarded them for a short while and then said, 'I have absolutely no idea. When I opened the door there was nobody there. Perhaps someone is playing a prank on us.'

Dylan stared at his father in confusion while Sandra's face turned serious when she replied, 'Well, you won't mind me checking then, will you?'

'Go ahead, honey,' said Jayden, 'I have nothing to hide.'

She rushed downstairs and opened the door, poking her head out and gazing around. 'Who's there?' she said loudly, walking out onto the porch in her silk nightgown, waiting for her eyes to adjust to the darkness.

Jayden had followed her down the stairs and was now standing in the doorway. 'Come inside, Sandra. It's freezing out there,' he said, sounding concerned.

She hugged herself against the cold, then shook her head and stepped back inside. Jayden put his arm around her shoulders. 'You were right,' Sandra admitted. 'It must have just been someone playing games with us.'

As they walked back up the stairs beside each other Jayden said, 'Let's go back to sleep now, love. Dylan needs to go to school in the morning and we both have a big day at work.'

Dylan's worried face turned into a smile. 'Live to work, Dad,' he announced.

'Work to live, son,' Jayden replied after a nervous chuckle.

Sandra beamed as she escorted Dylan back into his bedroom before returning to her husband in the master bedroom.

'Goodnight, honey,' Jayden said, climbing into bed.

'Goodnight,' Sandra responded automatically.

Once the lights were out, Jayden turned his back on Sandra, in order to watch the alarm clock. He started making fake snoring noises and it wasn't long before his wife fell into a deep sleep once again. Jayden lay as still as he possibly could, controlling his breathing and counting down the seconds until it was time to go. After forty-five long minutes had passed, he silently sneaked out of bed before pulling on his wizard-like nightgown.

He left the room and crossed the hallway on his toes, then made it downstairs and went out through the back door.

Upon observing his friend stepping out, Steven called, 'Jayden!'

'Shhh,' Jayden whispered with a finger pressed to his lips. 'Please keep your voice down. We don't want to wake my family.' He approached Steven and took hold of his arm. 'Follow me,' he said, still whispering.

Steven tailed him into the small wooden garden shed at the far end of the yard. Once inside, he noticed two folding chairs, positioned around Item 101's nucleus, which was glowing on the floor.

★★★

Meanwhile, back in the house, the phone suddenly started ringing.

Sandra Carter awoke in shock for a second time in under two hours. She fumbled for the bedside lamp, eventually managed to switch it on, and then saw that her husband wasn't in bed. 'Jayden!' she shouted. 'Where are you?'

This commotion (the phone as well as her shouts) caused Dylan to also wake up in his room next door.

'Mummy!' he cried. 'The phone is ringing. Aren't you going to answer it?'

Sandra hopped out of bed and ran into Dylan's room in a panic. 'The phone is the least of my concerns at the moment,' she told her son. 'Daddy's gone!'

'What?' Dylan said with trembling lips. The phone stopped ringing for a brief moment, then started again. Poor Dylan began to cry.

'Wait here, darling,' Sandra now said. 'Everything is okay. Mummy's going to find out why all these strange things are happening to us, all right?' Dylan nodded his head while wiping tears from his cheeks.

Sandra went downstairs and picked up the phone's handset. 'Hello,' she said cautiously.

'Hello?' A velvety female voice replied. 'Who is this?'

'You called me,' Sandra said, agitated. 'Who is this?'

'My name is Vanessa,' the other woman introduced herself. 'I'm Steven Leviki's wife.'

'I think you have the wrong number,' Sandra informed her. 'We don't know anybody by that name.'

'No, it's not the wrong number. I'm calling because I want to speak to Jayden Carter.'

'Well, Jayden's not here!' Sandra snapped. Then a frown formed on her forehead and she asked, 'How do you know Jayden?'

'I don't know Jayden,' replied Vanessa. 'I'm calling because my husband, Steven, has gone missing. I found a business card Steven had received from Jayden at some point.'

'Why do you need to speak to my husband then?' Sandra inquired. 'Is Steven one of Jayden's patients?'

'No, he's not. I think Steven is with Jayden at this very moment. I have a feeling our husbands are doing something secretive behind our backs. Something they aren't telling us about.'

Sandra thought about this for a moment. 'Hmm,' she said, more to herself than to Vanessa Leviki. 'So that's why Jayden has been acting so weird lately.'

'Steven's been acting weird recently, too!'

'Feel free to come over my house at any time,' Sandra offered. 'We can discuss it further and see if we can get to the bottom of this.'

'Okay, what's the address?' Vanessa said urgently. 'I'm coming over right now.'

CHAPTER 17
A SNAKE IN THE GRASS

Steven and Jayden sat on the folding chairs, facing each other, with the nucleus between them on the floor. They were both just staring at it, not speaking and not looking at one another.

After a prolonged moment of silence, Jayden eventually lifted his head and said, 'You know what we need to do, right?' He was slowly nodding his head, in an effort to convince Steven of the suggestion he had made earlier. Steven now made eye contact and also began to nod his head, almost hypnotically.

This carried on for a good two minutes before Steven said, 'Oh, I know, believe me.' He cautiously picked up the nucleus and then they both rose to their feet.

While peering at the device with squinted eyes, Jayden spoke in a low voice. 'I have a sledgehammer in here somewhere,' he told Steven. 'We could smash it to pieces.'

'I say we burn it,' Steven countered. 'That way we'll leave no evidence.'

Without warning, Jayden snatched the nucleus from his grasp and said, much louder, 'No chance, my friend. Burning it would attract too much attention to us.'

'There would also be a deafening noise when you smash something this hard, *genius*.' Steven replied sarcastically. He placed his hands on the nucleus and tried to pull it away from Jayden.

They grappled over the sophisticated piece of equipment for a while, as if in a tug of war. At some point during the struggle, Steven's hands slipped and Jayden gave a mighty pull, causing him to lose his balance. The nucleus slipped out and spun up into the stuffy air like a twirling missile. Without the presence of mind and too slow to react in order to catch the device on its downward path, they both watched (with mouths hanging open) as the nucleus landed on the floor, making a dull thud.

This was followed by a sharp snapping sound, as the tube holding the empty plutonium container cracked open. There was now a big gaping compartment in the nucleus and the tiny holes beyond the mesh of electrical wires began to emit white noise again. Like before, the piercing sound kept on changing pitch, going higher and lower while changing in frequency. Jayden, having experienced this already, was more prepared than his visitor. His palms were already clasped over his ears and he was gritting his teeth in fear.

'What's happening here?' Steven asked, gasping for air as he was trying to catch his breath.

The white noise then reduced to a low hum, whereafter a metallic-like voice announced, 'This is Professor Alberstein speaking. Come in, come in.'

'Listen to that!' Steven exclaimed. 'Did you hear that, Jayden?' His heart was thumping in his chest and he felt sweat trickling down the nape of his neck. Nevertheless, he bent down and shouted, 'Anybody there?'

Jayden's face turned pallid with shock. 'Why the hell did you speak to it, you fool?' he yelled. 'Do you want to get us killed?'

★★★

While this was happening in the garden shed, Sandra Carter was standing in the house with one ear pressed to the front door. Thankfully, her son had been able to fall asleep again in his bedroom upstairs.

She jumped, startled, when there came a sudden knock from the other side. Sandra ripped the door open to find the woman who had phoned earlier standing on the welcome mat. 'Hello, I'm Sandra,' she said. 'You must be Vanessa... You're taller than I expected,' she added as an afterthought.

Vanessa Leviki smiled drily. 'Yeah, that's why I never wear high heels. Nice to meet you, Sandra.'

Sandra invited her in and once they were seated in the living room, she said, 'I don't know what's going on with our husbands, but I suspect we'll have to put aside the fact that we are married to them and find out if they are up to anything illegal.'

'I fully agree,' replied Vanessa, interlocking her slender fingers on her knees. 'We have to act in a way that's best for the regime. I mean, following the regime's mandate is all that matters in this life. Steven skipped work the other day and that is breaking the rules we live for, isn't it?'

When she heard this, Sandra recalled that Jayden had also missed work recently. She folded her arms across her chest and said, 'And I don't know about you, Vanessa, but I have a kid to worry about. Our husbands need to be role models for their children, living to work, and working to live.'

'That's true. I don't want my kids to see their dad galli-vanting off, pretending to go to work when he's not.'

'Exactly,' Sandra concurred. 'Jayden has never lied to me before, and now all this.'

The two women gazed at each other for a short while before Vanessa said 'We should phone the hotline.'

Sandra sighed. 'You're right.' She stood up and walked to the telephone. Using the rotary dial, she selected three digits in sequence.

'Government helpline, Jonah speaking,' a voice answered. 'What is your emergency?'

After clearing her throat, Sandra said, 'Hello, Jonah. I would like to report a possible breach in regime rules. My husband, Jayden Carter, and his friend, Steven Leviki, have been acting very suspicious lately. They've been skipping work together, without any apparent good reason, and they've not been performing their family duties properly. Right now both of them are missing. We need someone to find them and follow them to figure out what is going on.'

'Thank you so much for your call, ma'am,' replied Jonah. 'We appreciate your honesty and we'll be sure to look into the matter as soon as we possibly can.' Once he'd hung up the phone, he looked at his superior and said, 'Raphael, we have a snake in the grass.'

Rafael knew exactly what that meant. He picked up the red telephone on his desk while mumbling, 'I'll get the supreme leader on the line.'

CHAPTER 18
EXECUTIVE AUTHORITY

'Don't listen to it and don't talk to it!' Jayden shouted to Steven. 'That voice might poison our minds.'

'All right then,' Steven replied tentatively. 'Let's destroy the thing before it can speak again.'

Jayden agreed but when he searched for the sledgehammer he'd mentioned earlier he couldn't find it anywhere in the shed. The two of them frantically rummaged through the shelves and the tool chests, and Steven eventually found a heavy steel crowbar. 'Will this work?' he asked Jayden, holding up the metal rod.

'Sure, let's do this,' Jayden told him.

As they were about to smash Item 101's nucleus to smithereens, the professor's voice came from it again: 'So, you've decided to keep the news of our existence to yourselves then? Why is that?'

Steven and Jayden looked at each other in disbelief. Their jaws dropped simultaneously and a gasp came from Jayden's mouth. Steven let go of the crowbar and it clattered to the floor. 'How... how did you know?' Jayden stuttered, glaring at the nucleus. He paused, then added, 'You must be a...'

'Genius, yeah,' Professor Alberstein finished the sentence on his behalf. 'Don't worry, I get that a lot.'

With wonder written across their faces, Steven and Jayden knelt down while regarding the alien device with envious eyes.

The professor's voice was now loud and clear. 'I have programmed the coordinates for the nucleus you are looking at to land in one of your citizens' hands for this exact reason. For you to make an informed decision by evaluating the consequences of life in another world. What would the implications be for your society to have knowledge of a different world to yours? A world called planet earth?'

'What do you mean?' Steven asked, frowning.

'What I mean,' replied the professor, 'is that this was designed as an experiment - call it a test if you like. And the mere fact that you are not fazed about extra-terrestrial life tells me that you fellows have passed the test.' There was a celebratory tone in his voice.

When neither Steven nor Jayden said anything in return, Professor Alberstein's voice said, 'So, what are you waiting for? Smash the damn experiment. The test is over.'

Steven picked up the crowbar and then turned to Jayden. 'Here, take it,' he said. 'You are an incredibly selfless person and you've saved our society. I want you to have the honours.'

'It would be my pleasure,' Jayden replied as he took the crowbar and stood up. He positioned himself over the nucleus with his feet planted wide apart and then squared his shoulders. Lifting the crowbar above his head, he realised that his teeth were chattering and his arms were trembling. 'Ready?' he shouted.

He was about to bring the crowbar down with tremendous force when a voice coming from the nucleus called, 'WAIT! You're making a huge mistake!' The voice was not that of the professor. This one was deeper and had spoken with much more urgency.

'WHAT?' Jayden yelled back, the crowbar still held firmly above his head

★★★

Back at Area 51, Professor Alberstein saw that it was the president who had barged past him to speak into the microphone. After he'd given the warning to Jayden from the other world, the president kept on talking into the microphone when he said, 'Guards, detain this man!'

A couple of muscled security guards stepped forward and grabbed the professor by his elbows.

'Let me go!' cried Professor Alberstein. The president covered the microphone with his hands while the professor continued to protest. 'You'll never get away with this!' he hissed through his teeth, glaring at the president with abhorrence on his face. 'You have no idea what you're doing!'

'Silence him!' the president ordered. The guards bundled the squirming professor to the ground and one of them shoved a cloth handkerchief into his mouth.

'Their society must be totally efficient,' Command Sergeant Major Earl now remarked, pointing at the mainframe's microphone.

'The rate of their advancement surpasses ours by light-years,' Fisher added.

Jared Williams nodded before saying, 'I agree. I think this is a threat, Mr President.'

Uncovering the microphone, the president spoke slowly. 'You are now hearing from the most powerful man on planet earth. I order you NOT to destroy the nucleus, do you hear me? You have to do the right thing and report its existence to your authorities.'

***

In the utopian world, Jayden Carter raised his eyebrows and his eyes widened in confusion, whilst Steven Leviki was looking at the nucleus as if it were poisonous, his face red with anger and frustration.

'Sorry, but our minds have been made up,' Jayden said. 'We will do what the professor asked of us.'

'You strongly need to reconsider your position, young man,' the president warned. 'Because, if you don't, I'll order a nuclear attack of massive proportions. An atomic bomb that will wipe out your entire existence.'

Horror appeared on Jayden's face upon hearing this threat. He dropped the crowbar to the floor and hunched down, feeling completely defeated.

Steven slumped down beside him and moaned, 'We simply cannot win.' Then the tears came.

'Life as we know it, is over,' Jayden stated. 'We need to prepare for the worst, Steven, my friend.' He took hold of Item 101's nucleus and pulled it to his chest. 'You did this to me!' he blurted out. 'You did this to *us*.' He then looked up at the ceiling and howled, 'TO ALL OF US!'

CHAPTER 19
THE HEART KNOWS BEST

'Open up!' a male voice suddenly shouted from outside the garden shed.

'Who's there?' Jayden replied, while slowly putting the nucleus down on the floor.

'We are government officials. Open this door immediately!' They were now trying to force the door open; the lock on the inside was rattling like a dozen wasps inside a tin can.

'What are we going to do?' Steven asked Jayden. His bottom lip was trembling and his eyes were darting back and forth between the door lock and the ominous nucleus.

Jayden scanned his surroundings and then indicated a large tool chest in the corner. 'Push that chest in front of the door,' he ordered. 'Keep them out until I have finished the job.' Steven did as he was told.

'We know you're in there!' one of the government officials shouted. 'Open up right away or we will break the door down.'

Jayden quickly wiped his sweaty hands on his nightgown, then picked up the crowbar...

★★★

Jared Williams, who was standing a few paces away from Earl and Fisher, glanced in their direction and noticed that they were totally engrossed in the situation unfolding around Item 101's mainframe. He gently approached them from behind and loosened the Velcro strip securing Fisher's shotgun to its holster. Fisher didn't even bat an eyelid.

Snatching the firearm in a swift motion, Jared aimed at the president while shouting, 'Everybody freeze! Stop right there!' He shifted his gaze to the security guards and said, 'Put your guns down, or I will shoot the president.'

'Do what he said,' the president instructed, nervously rubbing the back of his neck.

Everybody who was armed cautiously placed their weapons on the ground, then lifted their hands above their heads in surrender. Jared pointed his chin to where the professor and Carla were being held. Speaking slowly and loudly, he said, 'Let them both go, or the president will not see the end of this day.'

The guards released their grips and Professor Alberstein dropped to the ground. He stood up in a hurry and dusted himself off before walking over to the microphone. 'This is the professor,' he announced. 'I'm asking you to trust me now. Follow your heart. Do what feels right in your heart!'

Back in the shed, Jayden and Steven looked into each other's eyes and froze upon hearing Alberstein's croaky voice.

CHAPTER 20
IT'S OVER

All of a sudden, Jayden Carter knew his instincts had been right all along. With a nervous grin upon his face, he coiled back his arms and then brought down the crowbar with all the strength he could muster, bashing it into the nucleus. There was a piercing crack as the nucleus parted and split down the middle, exposing the thousands of tangled wires. As if it was somehow hurting, the nucleus began to produce white noise again, the sound bouncing off the walls in shrill streams. Jayden continued to smash it relentlessly, now screaming with fury. Eventually, after about three minutes, the nucleus – or what was left of it – went silent. The smell of burnt metal and rubber filled the air, and they were now standing in a cloud of thick, blueish smoke.

Jayden threw the crowbar aside, panting. He looked at Steven and placed a hand on his shoulder. 'For the greater good?' he said, then gulped to swallow down his earlier anxiety.

'For the greater good,' Steven responded, squinting his eyes. After Jayden had agreed with the next course of action, Steven unlocked the door and they stepped out into the cool morning air with raised hands.

Jayden regarded the four uniformed government officials standing in his backyard and said, 'Take us away.'

Without saying anything in return, the government officials handcuffed them and then escorted them through the house and into a police van out in the street. Jayden Carter wasn't afraid in any way, shape or form. He knew he had done the right thing. He had followed his heart, just like the professor from the place called planet earth had urged them to do.

★★★

Carla Williams raced over to her husband, jumping with joy. She embraced him snugly and then gave him a passionate kiss that felt as if it lasted a lifetime. When their lips finally parted, she caressed his cheeks with her fingers while saying, 'I love you so much, Jared.'

'I love you too, Carla,' he told her, stroking her hair. 'And I'm so sorry... for everything. I promise I'll right my wrongs. You deserve to be treated like a princess and I will be your prince, like I've always been.' He then turned his attention to Professor Alberstein and winked. 'I'm so sorry,' he said honestly.

'All is forgiven,' the professor replied, smiling brightly.

Jared dropped the shotgun to the ground, but as soon as he did Earl pounced on it and pointed the barrel to Carla and Jared. 'Permission to pull the trigger?' he asked the president, tightening his jaw.

Professor Alberstein started laughing uncontrollably.

The president sighed. 'Put the gun down,' he ordered in a deflated voice.

Earl let go of the weapon and Jared stared at the professor in mystification.

'The president knows that I'm too useful to the US government,' Alberstein said in clarification. 'And he also knows that I'll refuse to work with them in future if he kills the two of you.'

'You really are a genius,' said Carla. Her eyes were glimmering with delight. Behind her, a rainbow appeared over the horizon, seemingly out of nowhere.

'Why, isn't that just gorgeous?' Professor Alberstein said, making a canopy over his eyebrows with his hands.

They all turned around to behold the beauty of nature in the vast Nevada desert...